EDDIE
FANTASTIC

EDDIE FANTASTIC

By

CHRIS HEIMERDINGER

Covenant Communications, Inc.
American Fork, Utah

Printed in the United States of America
First Printing: August 1992
      96 97   10 9 8 7 6 5 4

Eddie Fantastic
ISBN 1–55503–403-9
Library of Congress Catalog Card Number: 92-071902

For Jim Walker
My dog-loyal fan and eternal friend

• PROLOGUE •

"Since you're new to this part of Salt Lake," began the gossipy ten-year-old girl from down the block, "I feel it's only fair to warn you. Nobody ever walks this street after dark."

"Oh, they don't, huh? And why not?" asked Eddie, tossing another shovelful of snow off the walk, failing in his best efforts to ignore the little brat. "Are there a lot of gang fights around here?"

"Nuh-uh. No gang has ever claimed this neighborhood as their turf—and for good reason."

"What's that?"

"The Lizard Man."

"The *who*?"

"The Lizard Man lives in this neighborhood. His house sits just over there—the one setting way in from the road with the high stone fence. Those barbs at the top are electrified."

"Why do you call him the Lizard Man?"

"Because he wasn't born with skin, like you or me. He has scales. And instead of fingernails, he has claws. Fangs hang down from his mouth, long and needle sharp, like a rattlesnake's."

Eddie laughed as he tossed another heap of drift. "Where'd you get such an imagination?"

"You don't believe me? I dare you to walk past there after midnight. Last fall a Laotian girl thought she could do it, too. That was the same night she disappeared."

"How old was this girl?"

"About your age. Fifteen."

"Sounds more like a runaway."

"That's what the police thought, too. But we who live in this neighborhood . . . we know better."

Eddie propped the shovel under his arm, enthralled by this girl's grasp of melodrama. "So what do *you* think happened to her?"

"The Lizard Man got her. He feeds after midnight, catching passers-by with his tongue when they wander too close to the bars on his tall iron gate. Part of the tongue always smothers the victim's mouth so they can't scream."

"Are you in any kind of therapy, little girl?"

"And then he eats them. Not all at once. He buries them in his cellar where the soil keeps them cool. He casts spells, too. Puts people in trances so they do exactly what he wants. Animals, too—"

"Have you actually *seen* this Lizard Man?" Eddie interrupted.

"Me? No way! I'm not dumb enough to go near the place—not even in daylight. But other kids have seen him, and they'll all tell you the same thing: He's not human."

Eddie was skeptical and once or twice, as winter turned into spring, circumstances even forced him to go by the place after midnight. He saw nothing, though admittedly he was riding a fast-moving ten-speed at the time.

• *ONE* •

One glistening spring afternoon toward the end of May, the day after the roller coasters began to thunder at Lagoon Amusement Park and the day before the wave pool began churning and splashing at Raging Waters, Eddie Fanta strolled in the door, having returned home from his last day in the ninth grade, and listened to his mother announce that the divorce was final.

There was a change in Eddie's expression, but it was barely perceptible. He nodded. The news was not shocking. It seemed to Eddie as natural a link in last year's chain of events as winter following autumn, or *Cheers* following *Cosby*.

Eddie knew his mother was hoping to see pain. She would be disappointed. The boy was immune. But Eddie's silence, the fact that he stood there, seemed to her a justified cue to pull the boy's silvery-blonde head into her shoulder and wait for a sob.

But Eddie's eyes remained unfocused. Cold. He found his mother's face and asked if he might have the leftovers from last night's sloppy joes as an after-school snack. While watching the cheese melt in the microwave, Eddie heard his mother in the front room retching the sobs he'd failed to provide. *Why cry now?* It made no sense. The divorce was *her* idea. She was the one who'd pushed for it. So Dad moved to Las Vegas to nurture another life with Michelle and two soon-to-be stepkids, ages six and eight, whom Eddie courteously referred to as the Swamp Things.

Eddie's mother cried a lot that summer, sometimes for no reason. And her drinking—a vice which had been latent since high school—grew steadily worse. Though she never drank in front of Eddie, it didn't take him long to key in on the hiding places: behind their lone box of food storage and between the mattress and box springs on her bed—on the side where his father used to sleep.

Eddie begged to spend part of the summer with his dad, hoping to salvage some of the promises he'd made the summer before; the one about conquering Mount Timpanogos, or camping Goblin Valley, or fishing Mirror Lake. But Eddie's mother said she couldn't be alone right now and assured the boy he could go to Las Vegas at Thanksgiving.

The last time Eddie had seen his father was in April, on Eddie's birthday. Dad took him to his favorite eat-joint, the Spaghetti Factory. On the way, Dad announced his impending engagement, which was to take place as soon as the divorce was final. Michelle met them in the waiting area, having arrived in her own car. She was brunette, petite, younger than Mom, though not as pretty as Mom had been. She talked a lot; and after the years of silence with Eddie's mother, Dad seemed to like hearing a woman talk.

Michelle had been briefed on Eddie's artistic abilities beforehand, and she offered compliments without having seen a single painting. After dinner, they drove separate vehicles to an indoor mini-golf course where Eddie met the Swamp Things, first introduced as Jesse and Brenda. They cheated, they whined, they made dents in the windmill with their putters, and when it was over, they called him *Eddie Soda Pop*—a nickname he hadn't heard since grade school.

When he arrived home, Eddie was halted in his tracks by a gust of liquored breath. His mother asked, almost accusingly, if he'd had a good time. He responded in the affirmative and made a beeline for his bedroom.

Safely inside, Eddie threw the latch on his self-installed deadbolt. Leaning against the door, he drew a deep breath and flipped on the lamps in each corner, with bulbs colored red, blue, green, and yellow. Laying back on his bed, he let the bedroom's images seep into his brain. All of them reached out to the ever more wonderful future. The wall was smothered with posters of planets and galaxies, nebulae and stars, sci-fi flicks and book covers, as well as his own watercolor creations of alien cities and landscapes.

An intergalactic dogfight was frozen over Eddie's bed, suspended by thin strands of fishing line—thirty ships in all, plastic models from *Star Wars*, *G.I. Joe*, and a half-dozen other fads. The center vessel was the largest, his favorite— the *Starship Enterprise NCC 1701-D*.

Pasted to the ceiling overhead were Eddie's heroes, Captain Jean-Luc Picard (or rather, a poster of the balding Patrick Stewart in his *Star Fleet* duds) and Captain Jacques-Yves Cousteau. Eddie wasn't sure why Cousteau was his hero. He'd seen a television special on him once—a birthday party or something—and he remembered being so awed that one man could accomplish so much in one lifetime: inventing aqualungs, constructing rescue subs, designing underwater cameras, writing books, exploring oceans, inspiring research foundations, and even becoming a famous television star. Cousteau had done more to advance his field than any man in history. When Eddie was old, with crow's-feet around his eyes, he hoped they'd do a birthday special on him, whatever might be the field he chose to advance.

While awaiting sleep, Eddie prepared his mind for another miserable year with befuddled adults at the helm of his life. He resented them all, although none more than his mother—the alcoholic author of his family's destruction. Had any worthwhile decision ever come from an adult?

Yes, Eddie remembered as he dropped off to sleep. *There was one adult I trusted. Grandpa Paxton.* Until Eddie was nine, his mother's wise and benevolent father had lived across the street. Some days, Eddie spent more time under his grandfather's roof than his own. The old man could make any animal you asked for with a single piece of paper folded a hundred intricate ways. He knew the secret ingredient to double-nut fudge and he'd thwarted the blow of a German soldier's bayonet.

On that terrible spring morning Eddie's mother asked no less than seven times if Eddie had done something to inspire Grandpa's stroke. Eddie insisted he was already like that when he stepped into the house. Did she believe him? Eddie wasn't sure. Just as well . . . because it wasn't the truth.

It took Grandpa two years to die. Eddie couldn't muster the nerve to visit the nursing home for nearly a year. When he finally did, the old man didn't recognize him. Eddie tried to go back every Saturday, helping his mother with her weekend job as nursing home custodian. But Grandpa never recognized his grandson again.

Eddie's life seemed divided in two: The days before Grandpa's stroke and those after. Days of stability, light hearts, and peace. And days of chaos, short tempers, and silence. When Eddie and his mother moved from their two-story home in Sandy, Eddie felt he was leaving his boyhood behind. The smells of the seasons, the views through the windows, the trails through neighbors' yards which led to the secret rendezvous points of lifetime friends: All these were gone forever.

Mrs. Fanta moved Eddie to a West Valley duplex in an unkempt neighborhood near Redwood Road. It was March, and though Eddie had begged to finish out the year at his old school, he was told it just wasn't "practical." As expected, all the cliques at the new school were decided back in September. Eddie's only hope for friendship was to find a person as new and out-of-place as himself. At the beginning of May, he found just such a person.

The opposite side of their duplex sat vacant all of April while the manager made renovations. In May, an Asian family moved in: A mother, a daughter, and a son. One afternoon, as Eddie hauled garbage out to the street, the son offered Eddie a hand and introduced himself as Lu-duc Ho.

"—but you can call me Duck," he added. "That what everyone call me back in Seattle."

Duck was a thin boy with darting eyes. His accent made it obvious he wasn't Seattle-born.

"Where are you from?" Eddie asked.

"You name it, that where I from," Duck replied. "Seattle, Guam, Thailand. I born in Cambodia. My family live there till I was eight. So tell me—any pretty girls live around here?"

Eddie felt uncomfortable at first, having lived all his life in a neighborhood where ethnic minorities were caged inside the walls of his television.

"What *kind* of girls?" Eddie asked, wondering if Duck's question should be limited to Orientals.

If Duck sensed prejudice, he didn't let on.

"Short girls. But still have long legs and like to show them. It also good if girl not know yet how pretty she is."

"Oh, that kind of girl," Eddie mused. "Good luck finding one like that around here."

Duck made a click inside his cheek and threw a snap off his fingers. "Darn. Seem like I always choose wrong neighborhood."

A smile climbed Eddie's cheeks.

The two of them spent the rest of the afternoon discussing everything from movies to moon walking. Eddie also convinced Duck to abandon his *Seattle Super Sonics* loyalty and adopt a higher appreciation for the *Utah Jazz*. When Eddie probed for details on Duck's voyage to America, the Cambodian recited a spine-tingling epic which included everything from communist murder plots to Malaysian pirates. Duck's older brother had died in a communist "reeducation camp." It took Duck's family two years to save enough money to flee.

It had been seven years since Duck's family heard from his father. The night Mr. Ho hid them all under blankets in a boat bound for Thailand was the last time Duck saw his face. The plan had been to meet at a specified place some days later, but Mr. Ho never arrived. The family struggled to stay in touch with relatives and friends in Asia who continued to pursue rumors, but so far, nothing panned out. Duck knew his father was alive, and he often dreamed of one day returning to Southeast Asia to find him.

Duck's stock of stories seemed endless. Eddie suspected he was embellishing at times; but even so, it was clear that this Cambodian's first fifteen years of life were infinitely more interesting than his own.

While in Seattle, Duck's family became Latter-day Saints. That's what brought them to Salt Lake. Mrs. Ho wanted to see a prophet. Duck found all this Mormon stuff dreadfully boring. He didn't share the same enthusiasm for this new religion as his mother and sister. He went to church because he was forced to; and for the first couple weeks, he begged Eddie to tag along.

But Eddie hadn't attended church since he was nine—the year things started to sour between his parents. He had no time for religion. Primarily because religion seemed to have no time for him. When he was too young to know any better, Eddie somehow developed an image of God as a kind of fireman with a white hat and white robes—a fireman from the sky who came down to rescue little kids from every possible danger. Now that he was older, he knew such ideas were foolish. God had never come down to rescue him from anything. Religion must give comfort to some, Eddie supposed—those who couldn't face the dark. But Eddie was no coward. He could accept the world at face value.

His father was said to be rekindling LDS affiliations in Las Vegas. This made Eddie uneasy. The Sunday afternoons he'd spent with Dad seeing movies or exploring remote mountain highways were some of his favorite memories. Eddie's secret fear was that Dad would change, seek a fresh start on a shiny clean slate and toss aside everything having to do with his failed marriage, including the son it had produced.

Duck wiled away many hours telling Eddie stories, but the Cambodian was actually much more interested in his new friend's love life.

"How many girls you kiss?" Duck inquired one day as the two rode bikes to 7-11 for Big Gulps.

"That's kind of personal, isn't it?" Eddie replied.

"Not that many, eh?"

"No! It's just . . . well, how do you mean the question? Are we talking about females in general or—"

"You change subject!" Duck accused. "We talking about *girl* girls. Not your mother!"

"There was Barb Brockman."

"How many times you kiss her?"

"Three times. Once each night, three nights in a row. We did a scene together at my old junior—"

"You mean you kiss her in play?"

"What's the matter with that?"

"It not count! Teacher *made* you kiss her."

"I didn't object."

"No, it still not count."

"Once in first grade a girl kissed me when I wasn't looking."

"That not count either."

"Then none!" Eddie scowled. "Are you satisfied?"

Duck slapped his hand to his chest. "Whew!" he breathed. "I thought I was only one!"

The relief they felt upon discovering this common failure in wooing women was only temporary. In three short months, they were bound for Jordan View High School. Eddie knew well the shame which could be heaped upon a member of his gender if he entered such an establishment without some kind of female success story. Some of his friends back in Sandy had already boasted a dozen girlfriends. Eddie Fanta had never even asked one of these oddly curved creatures out on a date.

Though she no longer attended church, his mother still adhered to the Latter-day Saint policy of having offspring wait sixteen years before dating. Outwardly, Eddie mourned the policy. Inwardly, he counted on it desperately. The rule protected him, gave him an easy excuse if someone pressed the matter. Then, one evening, shortly after his parents' separation, Eddie brought up the subject of dating just to make conversation and found himself reeling with the news that his mother was no longer firm on the issue.

"If you want to date, then date," Mrs. Fanta announced.

Eddie decided he'd keep this news under his hat—at least until he figured out what to do with it. Lu-duc Ho, on the other hand, unknowingly encouraged Eddie to face this challenge head on.

"Let's make bet," Duck suggested. "First one to kiss girl must pay other ten bucks."

"Make it twenty and you've got a bet," Eddie countered. "But the other one has to witness the kiss—*on the lips.*"

"And it must be longer than three seconds," added Duck.

"Three seconds!" Eddie counted the time in his head. *Wow!* "Let's not make this too complicated."

"Okay then. Just on lips. But girl has to kiss back."

"Deal!"

Eddie and Duck passed the summer wandering the midway of Valley Fair Mall and riding the slides at Raging Waters. 'Twas the season of girl watching. Eddie's eyes were busier than any summer in memory. Over the next three months he developed more crushes on more girls than in his whole cumulative life. Most times the infatuation lasted as long as it took to trail her from one end of the mall to the other.

But in late June, Eddie began to notice a certain heaven-carved blonde with glowing green eyes. He and Duck usually saw her right when the mall opened as she completed a mile or two of mall-walking with three other friends. Her makeup was always flawless. Fiery pink lip-gloss made her easy to spot from a distance.

Once in July she exercised late, finally eating lunch at the *Greek-ka-bob* in the Food Court. Eddie slipped behind her in line. As she was ordering, he unconsciously blocked the straw dispenser. She was forced to ask him to hand her one. As he did, she touched his knuckle, crooning "thank you" like an English princess. Her green eyes lingered a bit before turning away, giving Eddie all the hint he should have needed to make a move—join her for lunch—ask her to a movie—do something! But as usual, Eddie Fanta choked.

He carried his food to a nearby table to find Duck there shaking his head and clicking his tongue.

"Look like I keep my twenty dollar forever."

"How come *I'm* the show?" wondered Eddie. "I don't see you doin' much better."

"American girls not like scrawny Asians," Duck concluded.

"Sounds like a cop-out."

Duck grinned. "But it's a good one."

Eddie pointed out a threesome of Vietnamese girls at a table across the Eatery. "So go talk to one of *them*."

"They too old."

"No, they're not."

"They too young."

"*You're* too *chicken!*"

Before biting into his gyro, Eddie stole a glance toward the blonde girl's table. She was looking squarely at him, pretending at the same time to gab with her girlfriends.

And then she winked.

Eddie looked behind himself to see if the wink had been aimed at someone else. When he spun back, she was laughing. Her girlfriends were also giggling. Seconds later, they all stood up and left.

"That's the one," Eddie promised Duck. "That's the girl who'll earn me twenty bucks."

Eddie determined that the blonde girl mall-walked every Monday, Wednesday, and Saturday. This coming Saturday, Eddie was bent on asking this girl out on a full-fledged, genuine, honest-to-goodness date—and Duck wasn't going to miss this event for the world.

They got up earlier than usual, a whole fifteen minutes before eight. At five after the hour they met on the lawn and began the three-block trek to the bus stop. Duck had been so anxious to see Eddie make a fool of himself, he realized at midpoint he'd forgotten his bus pass.

Eddie groaned and leaned against the high stone fence along the sidewalk. "I'll wait. Run! We have to get there before the mall opens!"

Duck was off like a jackrabbit.

Eddie took this time to mull over his various methods of

attack. He'd opt for the "collision" approach: Act as though he didn't see where he was going and run smack into her. The date would be set while apologizing over a *Strawberry Julius*. Hopefully the collision wouldn't break any of her wonderful bones.

Eddie realized he was leaning against the stone fence of the infamous Lizard Man's lair. He smiled, recalling the tales he'd heard about this place when he first moved to the neighborhood. Eddie stepped over to look through the tall iron gate. This was the only place where you could see into the Lizard Man's yard, unless you stood on a neighboring roof. It wasn't the first time Eddie had peered into the property. He'd made it a point to look in every time he walked by, wondering if he might glimpse the legendary occupant. Thus far, he'd seen no evidence that anyone lived here at all.

The yard appeared as it usually did: grass unmowed, shrubbery thick and gnarled. The front door of the house was hidden under the heavy shadow of a screened porch. The view into the shadow was further obscured by its contrast with the bright morning sunlight.

Eddie squinted. It looked like there was a silhouette in the shadow, the silhouette of a man in a wheelchair, facing him, saying nothing. Eddie considered calling out "Good morning!" but the figure was too far away. Besides, it was too early in the day for yelling.

Eddie began to feel awkward, as if the silhouette was watching him. He was about to step out of the gateway when something new caught his eye. Eddie squinted harder, pulling his visor cap lower to shield out the glare. There was a tiny red light emanating curiously from the silhouette in the area of the figure's lap. Eddie wasn't sure if the light had been on all along or whether it had burst on as he was preparing to step away. At the moment he noticed it—that is, at the very moment it may have ignited—all the birds who'd been celebrating the morning with song, went mute.

Eddie glanced up at the trees and the telephone lines. Was it his imagination, or were all the birds facing toward the Lizard Man's house? And then—in perfect unison—every bird took flight, swooping down at the Lizard Man's yard like something out of a Hitchcock movie. Eddie's face went white. He witnessed them congregate on the sidewalk in front of the porch. There must have been a hundred and fifty of them, of every color and species. The birds organized themselves into tidy rows, with very little fluttering or moving about, as if some great bird god had called them together for an all-important meeting.

Eddie continued watching in trancelike awe as the screen door to the porch opened—all by itself! *Remote control?* And then Eddie heard a high-pitched rumble, like the scream of a snow blower, and a spray of birdseed shot out from within the shadowed porch, carpeting the lawn and sidewalk. A feeding frenzy ensued. Birds voraciously pecked and swallowed while Eddie waited anxiously for Duck to return. No one would believe only one witness!

As Duck's tiny frame came trotting around the corner at the end of the block, the red light flickered out. The birds, in response, took flight, again in unison, leaving the remaining seed untouched, seemingly forgetting what had made them swoop into the yard in the first place. Having found their old places on the branches and telephone wires, singing recommenced.

Eddie peered back into the shadowed porch, but the silhouette was gone.

"Let's go!" Duck's bus pass was now in hand.

Eddie's feet refused to move. His jaw still hung toward the sidewalk. He tried to tell Duck what he'd seen, but the words got fumbled and his Cambodian friend just couldn't understand what was so interesting about a man in a wheelchair feeding birds.

"Are you stalling so we miss bus?" Duck asked. "I *knew* you not go through with this."

"I'm coming." Eddie haltingly turned his gaze from the shadowed porch. "I'm coming."

• *TWO* •

She wasn't there.

For the next two weeks, Eddie and Duck faithfully boarded the eight-fifteen bus for the Valley Fair Mall in hopes of finding Eddie's green-eyed blonde. Every morning they met with disappointment.

"Maybe she and her friends find new mall to walk in," Duck suggested.

"Why would she change her routine? Did somebody tell her my plan?" Eddie gave Duck a double take, knowing him to be the only other human being aware of his intentions.

"Don't look at me!" Duck insisted. "I say nothing. Maybe we take bus to other mall—see if she walking there now."

"How could this happen?" Eddie mourned. "My first real love . . . vanished forever . . ."

Eddie and Duck continued to bus out to every mall in Salt Lake County—Fashion Place and Crossroads, Cottonwood and South Towne. But July became August and the first half of August became the latter-half. School would begin in less than a week and Eddie Fanta had yet to locate his green-eyed princess.

Every morning as he and Duck passed the Lizard Man's gate, Eddie would stop to gawk. But nothing unusual happened again. He began to wonder if anything unusual had *ever* happened. Strange, the tricks your mind can play when you're head over heels for a dame.

It was the final weekend of summer vacation. Eddie accepted the possibility of never knowing true love again. The image of emerald eyes and pink-gloss lips would haunt him the rest of his days. Even worse, Eddie and Duck would enter Jordan View High each having failed to win their own bet. There was only one way to ease such stresses—a final summer dunk in the wave pool at Raging Waters.

The water park was as packed as one might expect the last weekend before school begins. The wait to ride the H_2O Roller Coaster was an hour. Even the line for the Acapulco Cliff Dive was twenty minutes. The wave pool was standing room only.

All summer Eddie had tried to match Duck's tan. Here at summer's end, Eddie had to concede his defeat. Every time his skin achieved a slightly browner hue, Duck still had him one shade better. Nevertheless, Duck was impressed.

"Eddie, you lucky you not get skin cancer," Duck commented as the two of them waited in line for the highest tube run. "Wait'll next summer, Mr. Ho," Eddie replied.

A voice called from behind. "Eddie?"

Eddie felt a clammy hand on his shoulder. He turned to face a red-headed female in sunglasses.

"Eddie Fanta!" the girl repeated. "Don't you recognize me?" When she took off the shades, her identity sent a shock wave through Eddie as if he'd taken a bite of aluminum.

"It's me! Monica! From Eastmont!"

It was her all right. Monica LaRoche. The girl whose only ambition in life since the fourth grade was chasing Eddie Fanta. Actually, in junior high she seemed to have lost interest. But even then Eddie wouldn't take any chances. He'd peered around corners all three years at Eastmont just to be safe.

"Sure. Monica. How are you?"

"Great! I haven't seen you since February. I heard you moved away."

"Well, I didn't move far. Just to West Valley."

Monica gasped and slapped her hand to her mouth. Her body language always seemed exaggerated and affected when she got around Eddie. "You're *kidding*! My dad got a job at American Express. We moved out here in July. What a coincidence!"

"Yeah, what a coincidence," Eddie repeated flatly. Couldn't he escape this girl? Eddie blamed this very female for his late start in the social scene. In fifth and sixth grades, when Monica's antics to win Eddie's attention reached their most embarrassing pinnacle, his friends would rib him so bad he was afraid to show up for class.

"So are you going to Jordan View?" Monica asked.

"Yes," he said coldly. "I am."

"That's *great*! I was beginning to think I'd never see you again, Eddie Fanta."

"Yeah . . . so was I."Eddie glanced around, hoping to spot a hidden camera. It was amazing enough when Monica followed him to the same junior high considering Eastmont wasn't even in her district. Now she was following him to the same high school—*clear on the other side of the valley!*

"Well, it's good to see you again," Eddie said, wrapping up the conversation.

"Yes, it is."

Eddie turned away.

It was clear Monica had wanted to ask him a host of other things. She was likely undergoing some of the same adjustment pains Eddie had experienced when he moved here, leaving old friends and such. But she caught the hint. It was awkward pretending to ignore each other while waiting for the line to reach the top. What a relief when it became Eddie and Duck's turn on the slide.

After the ride, Eddie snatched up his tube and fled the water.

"What's a matter?" asked Duck.

"That girl!" Eddie exclaimed. "We've gotta get outta here or she'll follow us everywhere we go until the park closes."

"Is that bad? She look sorta cute."

"Cute? Monica LaRoche? Duck, if you'd known her for as long as I've known her, you'd change your opinion *fast*." Eddie explained on the way to the wave pool. "In elementary school we called her Monica the Roach. She used to wear these grandma dresses, like from pilgrim days. And she was such a klutz. Her legs were always covered with scabs. We watched her pick at them when the teacher was lecturing."

"That disgusting!" Duck conceded. "How old was she?"

"Eight or nine. But those scabs—the trickle of blood down her calf . . ." Eddie shuddered. "Those are images you never forget. She used to write me love notes about how I was in her dreams at night. About how she wanted to marry me and take me to some deserted tropical island. The envelope always had five or ten kiss marks—each one with a different colored lipstick."

"That not sound so terrible."

Eddie thought about it. "Well . . . maybe not if I was to get such letters *today*; but in the fifth grade, it was pure horror."

"She seem nice now. Maybe she your best chance to get my Andrew Jackson."

"Duck, I'd need a lot more than twenty bucks to kiss Monica the Roach."

And with that, Eddie dove into the only open spot in the deep end of the wave pool. The pool was calm when Eddie entered the water, but while propelling himself across the bottom, the wave machines kicked in and Eddie's body twisted in the currents. Poking his head out of the surf, Eddie discovered he'd only made it halfway across—exactly the worst place to be when the waves started churning, especially when his tube was at poolside. Eddie spun around, preparing to kick furiously back to the edge. As he scanned the shoreline for Duck, his eyes halted on a sight considerably closer.

Four feet before his nose, splayed back in the sun like an aquatic goddess, was the green-eyed blonde, blissfully floating aboard her own innertube, rising and falling with the waves. It was amazing how her makeup seemed ever frozen in magazine-ad perfection. A wave immersed Eddie's head before he was fully convinced the vision was real. When he tread to the surface again, the girl's eyes were locked into his.

"Need a hand?" she asked.

Eddie spat a gulp of water and nodded.

"Grab on," she invited.

Eddie paddled forward, draping an arm over her tube. He hung there a moment, unable to speak, unable to breath.

"What's your name?"

"My name? Uh, that's . . . uh . . . Eddie. My name is Eddie."

She laughed. "I'm Tanya." Squinting coyly, she shook her finger at him. "I've seen you around before. Where was it?"

"The mall." Eddie answered a little too quickly. "We used to . . . I mean, *you* used to walk there. We were in line together at the Greek-ka-bob."

"Thaaat's right. You gave me a straw."

"Yes, I did. Was it okay?"

"Oh, yes. It worked fine."

One of Tanya's friends on a nearby tube called over, "You're playing with fire, girl."

"So I like to live dangerously!" Tanya called back. She faced Eddie again, speaking as if still to her friend, yet her purr was loud enough for Eddie's ears only. "Besides, this one is *cuuute.*"

"It's easy for *you* to live dangerously," the girl called over again. "But what about *him*?"

"Is something the matter?" Eddie asked.

"Oh, Gwen is just worried that my old boyfriend might see you hanging on my tube. He gets *very* jealous." She cupped her hand under his chin. "But you'll protect me, won't you?"

Eddie looked to the pool's edge to see if some muscle-bound hulk was fuming down on them. All he could see was Duck, dangling his legs over the side, waving.

"This guy is your *old* boyfriend?"

She nodded. "We just broke up. He went to ride the H_2O Roller Coaster and sulk."

This moment was as good as any. Eddie cleared his throat. "What would you think . . . I mean . . . would you like to go to a movie or something?"

"A *movie*! Oooooo, the date of my dreams! How old are you, Eddie?"

"Uh, seventeen," Eddie lied.

"Seventeen! A whole year older than me. What school do you go to."

"Well, I'll be . . . I mean, I'm *going* to Jordan View."

"What do ya know? That's where *I* go! How come I've never seen you before?"

"I like to lay low."

"I see. So are you going to pick me up for this date or should I meet you there?" She grinned and glanced at her friend.

Eddie was shocked. "You mean you'll go out with me?"

"Of course, I'll go. How could I turn down such a strong, handsome little boy like you?"

Eddie blushed. "Yeah," he replied.

Tanya lifted an eyebrow, still waiting for an answer to her previous question.

"Oh! Uh—maybe we should meet there," said Eddie. "My car's in the shop right now."

"Mmmm. I understand. So is this date for tonight?"

"I guess so."

"Oooo, I can't wait. I suppose we'll be going to a dollar movie?"

"Sounds good to me," said Eddie, trying to lace 'kool' into his voice. "How 'bout the seven o'clock showing? And don't worry—I'll be paying your way."

She gasped. "You're so generous and kind."

At that moment the wave machines quit and the pool grew calm.

"So until tonight then, my knight in shining armor," Tanya whispered.

Eddie was mortified by what happened next. Duck wouldn't have believed it either, if he hadn't witnessed it from shore. Tanya reached forward, molding her hand around the back of Eddie's head. Her eyes closed to a seductive slit and her pink-gloss lips moved carefully forward. Their lips touched, lightly at first, and then she pulled him in tight, spreading lipstick over and around every inch of his mouth. She released him with a loud smack and let the boy, his face now smeared with a bright circle of pink, slip slowly under the water.

*   *   *   *

"Now *that* what I call earning twenty bucks!" Duck handed over the money. "I never *see* someone earn twenty bucks the way I just see *you* earn twenty bucks. I surprised you not need a respirator."

Eddie continued to pace his bedroom. Duck lounged regally on Eddie's bed.

"You've got to help me, Duck. What should I wear? What am I supposed to say?"

"Say same things you did this afternoon. It work pretty well."

"I sounded like an idiot . . . actually, I don't remember *what* I sounded like. It's all a blur." Eddie stopped pacing and faced Duck. "Do you really think she likes me?"

"It look that way very much from where I sitting."

"It did? She did kiss me, didn't she . . . but I wondered if she was making fun of me at times."

"That how girls act to hide shyness."

Eddie slumped down on the bed, sitting at Duck's feet. "Heck, maybe she won't even show up tonight."

"Best advice I give you," said Duck, "be yourself. She either like you—deep psychological problems and all—or she not worth it anyway."

"Good advice." Eddie took several deep breaths, blowing out slowly. "Thanks, Duck."

Duck noted the clock. Five-thirty. "I best let you get ready." He climbed off the bed and made his exit. "Good luck, stud."

Eddie toiled for the next thirty minutes before the bathroom mirror. Tonight was the excuse he finally needed to open the bottle of *Stetson* his aunt had given him for Christmas. He also smeared gel in his hair for the first time since grade school graduation and buried every pimple under a dot of his mother's foundation.

His mother was just tucking a pizza into the oven when he stepped out wearing his 501's and a yellow-black, button-up shirt. She was slightly stunned. "Wow! What's the occasion?"

"I have a date."

Mrs. Fanta's shoulders drooped a little. "A date? With who?"

"Nobody you know."

"Who said you could start dating?"

Eddie was afraid of this. Sometimes his mother had a memory as long as a hangnail.

"*You* did! A couple months back. Remember?"

"I remember no such thing. I've put in a pizza. I've rented a movie."

Eddie noticed the video on the counter. "Mom, I've seen *Somewhere in Time* about five hundred times. What am I supposed to do? Stand her up?"

"Don't whine at me. I just think we should discuss this."

"There's no time. Our date is at seven."

"We've always said you wouldn't start dating until you were sixteen."

Eddie grew stern. "Mom, I *swear* you said it was *okay*! Were you drinking at the time? Is that why you can't remember?"

His mother stiffened. Eddie felt bad. Still, he couldn't believe she was looking so shocked. *Does she actually think I don't know? How stupid does she think I am?* After a moment his mother turned back to the oven and twisted the knob around to broil.

"Go," she quietly consented. "You'll be late—"

When she turned, Eddie was already gone. Mrs. Fanta heard the front door open and shut. She closed her eyes, biting her lower lip the way she did as a kid when a sliver was being pulled from her thumb. A moment later she found herself in the corner chair of the darkening living room. By the time she remembered the pizza, it was too charred for consumption.

*   *   *   *

Eddie arrived at the Valley Fair Mall at a quarter to seven. Quickly, he weaved his way down the midway. But he couldn't go *too* fast. It was very important not to have sweat dripping off his nose when he stood face to face with Tanya.

At the ticket booth of the Valley Fair Movies Nine, he was grateful Tanya hadn't arrived. The line was long, it being Saturday. The only show without a "Sold Out" banner was *Robin Hood*. It didn't start until seven-thirty, which Eddie felt might work out perfectly in case Tanya opted to be fashionably late, as he'd heard women were prone to do.

Eddie bought the tickets and grabbed a table in the Food Court, which faced the mall's east entrance. With his Reeboks kicked up on the neighboring chair, he eagerly waited for his princess to make her appearance. What would she be wearing? Something sensuous, he was sure. Would he get another kiss that night? Maybe he'd date this girl all through high school, take her to his senior prom, and marry her shortly after graduation.

When Eddie snapped back to reality, the clock inside the ticket booth read seven twenty-five. Eddie arose and looked around. The ticket line was shorter. Patrons were already buying tickets for late shows. The outside doors were free of traffic, no one coming or going. Leaning left of the entranceway were a pair of older boys with flat-top haircuts. The crown of their heads had been bleached, then dyed a rusty-red on the very tips. One wore parachute pants and a red mesh shirt. The other had bright yellow suspenders and a T-shirt torn off at the pecs. Both wore sunglasses, despite being inside. Eddie chuckled quietly. He used to wonder if he'd ever join a gang. Definitely not if they were forced to wear such ridiculous hairstyles.

Eddie realized he'd never really told Tanya a specific meeting point. She could be waiting for him anywhere in the vicinity. He jogged to the other end of the Food Court, looking both ways down the midway for a flash of those pink-gloss lips. She was nowhere in sight. Eddie sighed and went back to his table, slumping into the chair.

"I've been stood up," he muttered under his breath. "My very first date and the hag stood me up."

Eddie looked out the east doors one final time. The gangsters were in the same place, only they'd removed the sunglasses and were staring back. Eddie had to agree with them. He did look awfully pathetic here by himself.

Heartbroken, Eddie wandered back through the Food Court and into the midway. *If she didn't like me, why did she kiss me? I'd always been told women were hard to figure out. Guess this is my first taste of what's ahead.* Eddie exited the mall and crossed the parking lot. When he reached the bus stop, he planted himself on a bench.

Minutes later, the two gangsters from the Food Court plopped down beside him. A third gang member had joined them somewhere en route. This one also exhibited the unusual haircut with a crimson-dyed top, only he'd gone all out. His entire head had been bleached and the crimson dye bled down to his scalp.

"How are ya?" the new one called over.

"Good," Eddie replied.

Eddie fidgeted. Something about the boy's tone Eddie didn't like. At that moment, a long Buick pulled up behind them. It was an odd place to park, so far from any mall entrance. The windshield was tinted, so Eddie couldn't see the driver, only the bright yellow ash of his cigarette and the silhouettes of three or four passengers.

Eddie's blood pressure shot up. He didn't know why. *There's nothing wrong here—nothing wrong at all.* When his bus arrived he sighed, relieved.

"See you guys later," Eddie said and climbed aboard.

"Nice meeting ya," said the guy with a blood-red scalp. The one chewing gum let out a cackle.

Eddie slid into a seat near the front of the bus. A moment later, the three gangsters were dropping coins into the metal funnel beside the driver. They smiled at Eddie and claimed seats directly across from him. "Looks like we're headed in the same direction," smiled the blood head. He locked his knuckles behind his head and kicked out his feet, his heel leaving a guff-mark in the bus floor grime.

Eddie didn't reply. But after the bus left the mall and made its way toward Redwood Road, Eddie glanced out the window and noticed that the long Buick was tailgating the bus—following them! When the bus driver pulled over for a stop, the Buick drove ahead half a block and waited.

"What's going on?" Eddie asked the gangsters.

"Nothin'," the blood head innocently responded. He lifted his brow at the others. "Anything goin' on with you guys?"

"Not a thing," they replied.

Eddie's heart threatened to beat a hole through his chest. When the bus arrived at his stop, Eddie exited quickly and *prayed* he'd be exiting alone. Unfortunately, Eddie heard the gangsters' heavy footsteps following right on his tail.

Without looking back, Eddie strode rapidly toward his house. Daylight was fading. The oak and birch boughs filled the street with twisted shadows. Eddie had closed the gap between the bus stop and his house by nearly a block when the footfalls moved in. He was passing the high stone wall of the Lizard Man's yard, ready to break into running, when two of the gangsters grabbed his shoulders.

"Get your hands off me, man!" Eddie yelled, trying to alert the neighborhood. But the place remained as still as a churchyard. "What do you want from me?"

"We jus' wanna talk to you," answered blood head. "Calm down. Everything'll be fine."

The Buick screeched to a halt in the gutter beside them. Four more copper-topped gangsters sprang out of the car and surrounded Eddie on all sides. Most of these boys were Hispanic. However, the biggest one, the one who'd been driving—the one who stood over Eddie now—might have passed as one of Hitler's youth except that his hair wasn't truly blonde. It had a strong tint of red—a *natural* copper-top. A gold earring dangled from his lobe and a Harrison Ford-style scar crossed his chin. Over his right hand he wore what appeared to be a black racquetball glove with pointed silver studs. Carefully pinched in his left hand by all five fingers was a cigarette. He savored one final drag and flicked it onto the sidewalk, where he dutifully crushed it under his boot.

"So you must be Eddie. I've heard a lot about you, Eddie. Allow me to introduce myself. My name is Mikey."

"How do you know my name?" Eddie demanded.

"Tanya told me."

Eddie scowled. "What have you done to her?"

The gangsters laughed.

"The question is, what have *you* done to *her*?" said Mikey. "She came to me this afternoon with tears in her eyes, claiming some boy rudely came on to her in the wave pool. I assume that was you."

"I didn't come on to her. If anything, she came on to me. She kissed *me*—not the other way around."

"Now, now. That's not the way she tells it."

"I *swear*, that's what happened."

Mikey turned to the boy with the blood-red scalp. "Is that what happened, Miguel?"

"No, he kissed her," Miguel smirked. "I was there. I saw the whole thing."

"You're a liar," Eddie seethed.

Miguel, in a flare of temper, lunged forward, but Mikey held him back. It almost seemed rehearsed.

"Calm down, Miguel. Just calm down." Mikey turned back to Eddie. "You're making enemies awfully fast. Maybe you should start telling the truth."

"I swear to you, I . . ."

Slowly, Eddie shook his head. There was nothing he could say. Whatever they were planning wasn't negotiable.

Mikey sighed, "You disappoint me, Eddie. Tanya is a Copperhead girl. You should *know* that."

"I'm sorry. I didn't know."

Mikey set his hand on Eddie's shoulder, overcome with what appeared to be compassion.

"I believe you. I truly do. These kinda mistakes can happen so easily. And I can see by your face that you really *are* sorry, aren't you?"

"Yes, I am," Eddie whimpered.

"That means a lot to me. Unfortunately, Tanya sees this as an issue of pride. You see, you insulted my girlfriend and if she finds out I didn't do anything about it, she'll get terribly upset. Cry, throw a tantrum—who knows *what* else. To make things right between me and her, I'm going to have to hit you once . . ." He held up a single finger, then thought again and stuck two more fingers into the air. ". . . No, *three* times. Is that agreeable? Then we can call this whole thing even and go our separate ways."

Eddie looked for some flash of humanity—something which hinted that this was all a joke. Mikey's eyes were burning, almost glowing.

The gangsters tightened their grips on Eddie's shoulders. Mikey's fist—the one with the spiked glove—wrapped into a ball and his arm cocked for launching. Eddie stiffened as the Copperhead leader, sporting a toothy grin, propelled his fist into Eddie's left eye. The moment it hit, the gangsters released Eddie's shoulders, giving gravity a turn. Eddie fell back against the Lizard Man's iron gate. He crumpled to the ground, catching himself on his palms. The punch impacted his nose as well as his eye. He watched his own blood drip spots on the sidewalk.

Despite the gangsters' frenzied hooting and despite Mikey announcing, "That's one! Two to go," Eddie found himself in a bubble of silence. His eyes, almost involuntarily, turned into the bars of the Lizard Man's iron gate. Straining to see through the blur Mikey's punch had cast over his vision, Eddie followed up the Lizard Man's walk, past the buzzing porch light, and into the darkness beyond the front screen. No one was there—no silhouettes—but a strange feeling had settled over him. It was as if a harsh gust of wind struck his face, more penetrating than Mikey's punch.

Eddie knew he should have been thinking about his pain. He should have been dreading those two remaining punches. He should have had a million other worries and fears swirling in his head, but for some reason, he couldn't free himself from the unusual sensation which engulfed his mind as he gazed into the Lizard Man's lair.

"Can you get up?" Mikey's voice still reeked with mock compassion. "Do you need some help? Or would you like the last two strikes with my boot? Doesn't matter to me."

"Hurry up, Mikey," cried Miguel. "Leave some meat for us."

To Eddie, Mikey added, "We really must get on with this if everyone is to get a turn."

Eddie felt he had to almost rip his eyes away from the yard. Pushing himself to his knees, he glared up at Mikey and the other Copperheads. Slowly he started to stand, but one instant before his back was completely erect, Eddie's shoulder spun and his legs bolted forward. He broke through the mob and began charging toward his house at a speed his legs had formerly kept secret. The Copperheads were quick to pursue, but the gangsters' strides were no match for Eddie's adrenaline. Mikey hopped into his car to try and head him off. Eddie was already crossing the lawn of his duplex when the Buick's front tires jumped the curb and knocked over the Fanta's mailbox. As Eddie slipped inside, Mikey climbed out of the car and took a stance in the driveway. The other panting Copperheads gathered around him.

"You shoulda taken the last two punches, Eddie!" Mikey hollered. "That's what it'll read on your tombstone: 'If only I'd taken those last two punches!'"

A distant police siren pierced the night. Hastily, all seven gangsters pressed into the Buick. The car screeched away while Eddie watched through a slit in the curtain.

Eddie's heart continued pounding. His nosebleed had left the front of his shirt red and damp. Though he was gasping for breath and though his vision remained blurry, Eddie couldn't bring himself to think about his physical condition or even about his narrow escape. He was thinking about the Lizard Man's house. Something in that house had called to him. Something without a voice. It was still calling him now.

Delirious, Eddie thought. *I'm completely delirious.*

• *THREE* •

Eddie's mother had been sitting on her bed for twenty minutes.

She'd arrived home from work half an hour before, spent a few minutes trying to talk Eddie out of his bedroom, then retired to her own bedroom where she pulled the bottle out from under the mattress and set it on the nightstand. She'd been staring at it ever since.

Has it come to this? It's only a quarter past six. Am I already so eager to ease the pain?

Aside from personal turmoil, today had been a particularly hectic day at work. She'd messed up the billing on several accounts and lost two hours of time trying to straighten it all out. Her boss pulled her into the office and asked if there were "outside influences" affecting her work. She broke into tears and told him about the gang attack Eddie had suffered Saturday night. The story seemed to earn her boss's sympathies, though to Mrs. Fanta it was only the tip of the iceberg.

My son is right about me.

After Eddie had burst into the house Saturday night from the midst of threatening voices in the driveway, Mrs. Fanta of course, freaked out. What upset her further was when Eddie stopped her from flagging down the patrol car which had been summoned by some neighbor. It drove right on by the duplex.

"You don't know these guys," Eddie explained. "We could never cause them more trouble than they could cause us."

She lost her temper and regretted it later. Eddie was certainly experiencing enough pressure as it was. Still, she couldn't stop herself. She went on and on about all the stresses Eddie had heaped on her over the past few years.

"I can't trust you anymore," she ranted. "Ever since your grandfather's stroke you've lost all sense of responsibility."

At *that* point, *Eddie* blew up.

"Don't talk to me about responsibility, Mom. All I've got for an example is you! You say a person gets wiser as they get older. Well, you're twenty years older than me and your life is more bungled than any person's I know. What do I have to look forward to? I've got *your genes!* Does that mean the older I get, the more mistakes I make? Maybe it'd be better if I died now, while my life is only *partially* screwed up!"

And with that, Eddie fled to his bedroom, where he'd been ever since, except for when he got hungry or had to go to the bathroom. On Sunday morning, he detoured to tell his mother he was sorry for everything, but before she could reply, he'd thrown the deadbolt on his bedroom door.

The only visitor Eddie had on Sunday was Duck. His Cambodian friend had tried to come over the night before, just after the commotion, but he was turned away. Duck stayed an hour Sunday morning until Mrs. Ho arrived to drag him off to church.

Mrs. Fanta had wanted to question Duck as he was leaving, find out what her son was *really* feeling, but she changed her mind.

Wednesday, when Eddie goes back to school, I'm coming home during lunch to tear that deadbolt out of his door, she decided. Seeing the bottle again on her nightstand, she sighed. *What's to lose?* Before she could lift the neck to her mouth, the doorbell rang.

Duck was back. She directed him to Eddie's bedroom. Recognizing Duck's voice, Eddie unlatched the deadbolt and let him enter.

"You looking better," Duck commented.

Eddie's cheek and eye were still bright purple, but the swelling had gone down.

"Did you find out anything?" Eddie asked.

"Yeah, I find out a lot," Duck replied. "The guy who lead gang—the guy who hit your face—is Mikey Swearingen. He been leader of Copperheads for over a year now. Bad dude. Some say he kill people when he live in California."

"That's not what I'm talking about," said Eddie. "I mean did you find out anything about the *Lizard Man?*"

Duck dropped down on Eddie's bed. "Why you so curious about him? You should be more worried about Copperheads. This Lizard Man thing is obsession, Eddie. It not healthy."

Eddie climbed atop his desk chair to gaze out the window.

"Come here," he requested.

Duck did so. The chair supported them both.

"You see that?" Eddie pointed out the window.

"What?"

"That swamp cooler, sticking up from that roof over there. Beyond the trees."

"So?"

"That's *his* swamp cooler. That's the Lizard Man's roof. I *feel* something when I look over there, Duck. It's *weird!*"

"What you feel?"

Eddie stepped down. "I don't know. It's . . . I want to go there. *Badly!* I want to see what's inside. I want to meet the guy who lives there. It was the last thing I thought about when I went to sleep last night and the first thing that entered my brain when I woke up this morning. *Please,* Duck. I'm going bonkers over this! Did you ask anyone about him?"

Duck hopped down off the chair. "I ask some people at church. People who live in this neighborhood a long time. They say they know nothing about him, except his name."

"What's his name?"

"Louis Kosserinski. They say he crippled or something."

"That's all you found out?"

"They say only one man they know ever meet him."

"Who?"

"Brother Fayle. He one of the shut-ins. We take sacrament to Brother Fayle every Sunday. Nice man."

"Then you know where this Brother Fayle lives?"

"Sure."

"Let's go."

* * * *

It was less than two minutes by bicycle to Brother Fayle's front porch.

"So why is this guy a shut-in?" Eddie asked while pumping the pedals.

"He old. Have cancer," Duck replied.

"Is he well enough to talk?"

"Oh, sure. He just not leave house. His wife take care of him."

The Fayles' small yard was cluttered with ornamentation. There were not only bird baths and rock gardens, but Christmas lights—so many strings that taking them down after the holidays must have been too much effort. Sister Fayle answered the doorbell, her grey curls bouncing. She looked down at them under her glasses and smiled. But her expression changed when they asked to speak with Brother Fayle.

"Brother Fayle isn't doing that well today, boys," she responded. "Maybe if you came back in a week—"

"Who is it, Marie?" called a voice from within.

"Just some boys, Ray."

"Let 'em in!" Brother Fayle insisted. "I'm so bored I'm beginning to watch the pressure gauge on my oxygen tank for entertainment."

Brother Fayle had a bed on the living room couch. The cushions were permanently depressed, shaped by the old man's weight. A handy table supplied everything from magazines to pill dispensers. An oxygen tube was hooked into Brother Fayle's nose. His skin was ghastly white, and webby blood vessels had popped to the surface of both cheeks.

Sister Fayle led Eddie and Duck to chairs on either side of the old man and then retreated to the kitchen to prepare cherry Kool-Aid and Chips Ahoys.

Brother Fayle indicated to Duck. "Now, I've met *you* before. Brother Ho. Am I right?"

"Yessir," Duck confirmed.

"But I don't believe I've ever met this young man with the shiner."

"I'm Eddie Fanta. I, uh, got hit with a baseball."

"Do you go to our ward, Brother Fanta?"

"Well, no. My mother's not exactly active."

"So what's *your* excuse?"

Eddie considered being offended, but living in Utah, you got used to meddling Mormons. Besides, he asked with such frankness, the boy felt free to respond honestly.

"I'm not much for religion, I'm afraid."

"What about Scouts? Do you go to Scouts?"

"Uh, well . . ."

Brother Fayle turned to Duck. "Sounds like you better get this fellow out to Scouts, Brother Ho."

Duck simply nodded. He hadn't been to troop meetings either, but Brother Fayle had been ill too long to know.

"We'll get into this later," promised Brother Fayle. "Tell me, what's on your mind, boys?"

"We wanted to ask you about someone in the neighborhood," Eddie began. "They say you're the only one who's ever met him."

Brother Fayle's light-hearted tone mellowed a little. "Then you'd be wanting to know about Louis."

"That's right. Brother Kosserinski."

"Yes. I know Louis. Known him for thirty-seven years. His place was one of the first houses built in this neighborhood, back when most of West Valley was a swamp. What do you kids want to know about him?"

"We've never seen him," Eddie explained. "But we've heard stories—"

"Well don't believe them stories," snapped Brother Fayle. "I'm sure they're the same stories my children heard when *they* was little. Do you kids still call him the Lizard Man?"

Eddie nodded.

"I always thought that was a mighty cruel nickname. It'd be nice if you boys set an example and didn't call him that anymore. The fact is, Louis was in a plane crash a long time ago. Most of his body was burned, and he lost the use of both legs. His condition makes his skin sensitive to sunlight. That's why he never comes out much. He's also sensitive about the way he looks."

"How'd you meet him?" Eddie asked.

"I've been his home teacher for the last thirty-seven years. Up till this winter, I bought his groceries, mowed his lawn, and took the sacrament to him every Sunday."

"He's a Mormon?" Eddie asked.

"Darn good Mormon. His donations alone practically built our chapel and stake center. Always insisted on donating anonymously though."

Eddie looked perplexed. "Where'd he get the money?"

"Listen to me, my boy. Louis Kosserinski has more money than you or I will probably see in *two* lifetimes."

Eddie raised an eyebrow. *How did a crippled guy who never left his house acquire wealth?* "Did he sue someone way back when?"

"You mean 'cause of the accident? Nope. He was flying his own plane. He lost a ten-year-old son that day, too."

"Then where'd he get—?"

"Earned it. Louis was—*is*—an inventor. During World War II, he enhanced a lot of the radar and sonar equipment used by the Allies. After the war, he got into atomic energy, computers, microcircuitry, and other stuff that's way, *way* over my head. The royalties on his patents still pull in nearly a million a year."

Ducks eyes bugged out. "A million *dollars*?!"

"And that's only a fraction of what it used to be."

"And he lives in *this* neighborhood?" Eddie asked.

Brother Fayle chuckled, "If you saw the way his house was rigged up, you'd understand why he stays."

"What's he been doing since the plane crash?"

"Work. Man's a fanatic. Every time I'd go over there he was up to something or other down in that basement."

"He still invents things?"

"I suppose. I used to run errands and fetch parts for him twice a week. Was a time when he kept rats, pigs, dogs, monkeys—every exotic critter you can imagine. Back in the old days, he even had connections for gettin' human brains."

"You're kidding?" This guy really *was* a mad scientist.

Ray continued. "Once he sent me to the airport to fetch this new-fangled, high-tech doohickey flown in from Australia. I had to sign for it, so I saw the price tag. It cost him $365,000!"

"What was it for?"

"No idea. It was some computer gizmo about the size of one a them big screen TVs. The next day he signaled me to come over and haul it to the dumpster! The same computer gizmo! He said it turned out to be completely useless to him, so he stripped a couple circuits for spare parts and tossed the whole thing in the trash heap!"

"You shoulda sold what was left!" noted Eddie.

"I mighta thought about it if I'd a known what the dern thing was or who to sell it to. Besides, Louis has taken good care of my family over the years. I'd never 'a done somethin' behind his back."

"Where's the rest of his family?"

"Wife left him. It was right after the accident. There was another son, too. But I don't think he's ever heard hide nor hair from either one since."

Duck asked, "Who been helping him since you been sick?"

"No one. Louis never trusted nobody but me. And he used to get real ornery if I suggested bringin' somebody else over—even my own wife or kids."

"What about the last six months? Who gets his groceries now?" Eddie asked.

"No one I know of," said Brother Fayle. "But remember, he's a Latter-day Saint. The prophet said to get a year's supply of food and water, so Louis had me get him what must have amounted to a *three*-years' supply—for one man, that is."

"And he's been living on that all this time?"

"I guess so. He calls me now and then to ask how I'm gettin' along. I tell him I'll be on my feet and over to help him soon enough. Ain't that right, Marie?"

Sister Fayle had returned with the Kool-Aid and cookies. "That's right, Ray."

Eddie thought back on those days helping his mother at the nursing home before Grandpa Paxton died. Seemed like every time he went, there was a new empty bed. To Eddie, the ones who were close to the end all had a certain look. Brother Fayle had that look. He wouldn't be helping anyone anytime soon.

"What did you mean when you said he signaled you?" Eddie noted.

Brother Fayle sat up. "Say, now *that's* an interesting tidbit. He used to have this gizmo that measured electrical impulses in the brain. He explained it to me once, but I didn't follow a whole lot of what he was sayin'. He told me everyone's brains were basically a mish-mash of electro-magnetic somethin'-or-others—as individual as a man's fingerprints. He measured mine one day—that is, he recorded my brain print—and then he put the pattern into his computer. He told me if ever I felt a strong desire to come over and see him, he was probably sendin' me a signal."

Bingo! That's it!

Eddie pursued. "You mean he can put junk in somebody else's brain? Thoughts and stuff?"

"I guess so. I don't really know. All I know is, sometimes I'd get a hunch to go over there and he'd say to me 'Thanks for responding so fast, Ray.' I remember gettin' a big kick out of it. After thirty years, I guess it got to be old hat."

I knew it! He's "calling" me. But how? If brain prints are as individual as fingerprints, how did he get a hold of mine?

All this time Duck had been watching Brother Fayle's eyes grow more and more droopy. Sister Fayle finally noticed as well.

"I think you boys need to give him a rest now. You can come back and visit another day."

"But we were just gettin' acquainted," objected Brother Fayle, his voice starting to weaken and crack.

"It's fine," Eddie agreed. "We've learned a lot. Thank you."

"Well, I hope you boys'll spread the word about him," concluded Brother Fayle. "Don't you ever let anyone tease that man or make fun a-the way he looks. Just let him alone. Louis is . . . well . . . he's changed over the last few years. It'd be foolish to think a life like his wouldn't leave scars on the inside as well as the out. He'll be harmless if he's just left alone."

"But what if—?"

Eddie wasn't allowed to finish his question. Sister Fayle was herding them toward the door.

* * * *

Eddie and Duck gazed dauntedly into the expansive yard of the Lizard Man's—that is—of Louis Kosserinski's home. Their hands tightly clutched the cold iron gate as if they feared the ground might fall out from beneath their feet, leaving them hanging. There was no movement within. The shadows were long. It would be dark soon. Eddie thought about that and grew more nervous.

"Have you seen enough yet?" Duck asked.

"I'm going in," Eddie proclaimed.

"You crazy?" shrieked Duck. "Brother Fayle say let him alone. I say that good advice."

"You don't have to come if you don't want to," Eddie told Duck. "But I have no choice."

Duck pressed both hands to his forehead and mumbled a few frustrated words in his native language. He couldn't let his friend go alone.

Eddie looked at the latch. The rust blended right into the iron. This gate hadn't been opened all winter, maybe longer. Biting his lower lip, Eddie grabbed the latch. Its hold on the iron was stiff, but after a squeak and some fluttering chips of rust, it jarred loose. Duck helped push the gate open. The screech was horrible. All of West Valley could have heard! They expected a wheelchair to come barreling out the front door any second, its rider wielding a shotgun. But the door remained closed and the neighborhood fell back into silence.

"Okay," Eddie said, inhaling deeply. "Let's go."

Eddie led the way up the front walk with Duck pressing on his heels. They knew they were the first. No kid had ever stepped here before. Maybe there was a reason. Maybe this guy really *was* a psycho killer, just like that gossipy ten-year-old girl had proclaimed when Eddie first moved into the neighborhood. By the time they reached the screen door, Duck was ready to retreat despite his loyalties to his overzealous friend.

"We come far enough for one day, yes? Maybe tomorrow we go few steps further."

Ignoring the suggestion, Eddie asked, "Do you see a doorbell?"

Duck scanned the area. No doorbell was in sight.

"I guess we knock," Eddie decided and he lifted his fist, knocking to the tune of *shave-and-a-haircut, two-bits.*

The flimsy porch screen made his knock unexpectedly light. Eddie considered pounding on the siding, but it would have been virtually soundless and the knock might leave slivers in his fist. Eddie grabbed onto the screen door handle. Surprisingly, the porch wasn't locked.

"Eddie, what you doing?" whispered Duck, harshly.

"We have to knock on the front door itself."

"But this private property!"

"Not so loud!" Eddie whispered.

Eddie ascended the two lone steps leading onto the porch. Inside were dusty boxes, a pile of dusty newspapers, and what appeared to be the old shells of personal computer monitors. Quivering, Duck followed Eddie inside and the screen door shut behind them.

Some kind of mechanism had been built into the top of the screen door with wires running along the porch roof, disappearing into holes drilled into the house. *This must lead to the remote controller,* Eddie speculated. *The one he used to open the door that morning last summer.*

Something moved at their right.

Eddie and Duck scrambled as a darksome blur emerged

from inside a shell. A cat!—a big, fat, hairy one with white-tipped feet. Recognizing the animal as feline brought relief at first—then it became frightfully apparent this thing was nuts! Eddie had never seen a cat rear up so boldly. Every hair of its tousled coat was barbed—though not so sharp as its fangs—and it snarled and hissed like a viperous air gun. This creature thought it was a Bengal tiger! It sprang from a box, its claws fanned and loaded.

Duck staggered backwards out the door, saved from certain shredding by a pratfall onto the front lawn. Eddie tried to slip out to safety as well, but the cat captured his pant cuffs. After yanking free, Eddie barred the door shut behind him. It remained at the screen, flailing and spitting, furious to have missed an appetizer before dinner.

"I can't believe it!" Eddie exclaimed. "An attack cat!"

"Maybe it have rabies!" Duck suggested.

Eddie began laughing hysterically. A critter of nine or less pounds had driven them like a couple of hens. Surely one good kick would have eliminated the problem, but it had taken them by surprise. Duck failed to see the humor. "What you laugh about! We nearly get killed!"

Eddie laughed even louder. Then he noticed Duck was truly distressed.

"Ah, c'mon, Duck," Eddie consoled. "It's only a cat."

"That no cat! That Tazmanian devil!"

Duck arose and retreated briskly toward the gate.

"Where are you going?" Eddie called.

"Home!"

"Let's see if there's a door around back."

"You tell me all about it later!" Duck blew through the gate and disappeared behind the high stone fence.

Eddie looked back at the house, his eyes following up the rickety trellis with crispy-brown vines, past an aluminum-veiled second-story window, and up to the roof. No signs of life other than one crazy feline. But the "feeling" still pulsed in his head. Something inside this place dragged at him. He'd come this far. There was no turning back.

Eddie stepped around a corner where a storm drain seemed

fastened to the siding by wolf spider nests. He avoided a hedge of skeletal lilacs and approached the next corner. Somewhere there had to be another entrance—another place for his fist to knock. Yet how could the occupant have failed to hear all the racket? Maybe the owner was in another part of the house and since he was crippled, he'd been unable to reach the front door fast enough. Another door might be nearer to his location.

He found only one other entrance—an old-fashioned drop cellar door like the one Auntie Em jumped in when the cyclone was coming. Eddie dug his hand under the edge and lifted.

A boardwalk sloped downward, designed so a wheelchair could make its way up and out. Eddie tossed the door aside and descended. At the bottom of the walk, rising out of a bed of oak leaves, was another doorway. This one was steel with a tiny square window of foggy glass. *There's no way he'd leave* this *one unlocked,* Eddie speculated. Yet when he turned the handle, it clicked. The door fell open, slowly, almost on its own.

Eddie swallowed. Somebody might buy his excuse for entering the porch, but this was *definitely* trespassing. Trembling, Eddie Fanta entered.

At first he couldn't see a thing as his eyes adjusted to the phosphorescent lighting. But within a few seconds, it all became clear.

Wow!

All around him were the shapes and shadows of bulky equipment. Most of it was filthy, crusted with grease and oil, but some of it looked spit-polished clean with multicolored lights and terminals. There were three bright red laser beams emanating straight up from one machine captured by glass tubes coming down from the ceiling. There were pipes and wires and coolant gutters projecting everywhere. Eddie's feet kicked though a heap of metal chips.

A cross between a metal shop, Frankenstein's laboratory, and the engineering bay of the *Starship Enterprise*—that's how Eddie saw it. The basement comprised much more area than the house itself, stretching underground to either end of the property. There was a rail looping around to each separate work station and a host of pulleys and hydraulic lifters at locations where such was required. A crippled man didn't *need* legs here. In fact, legs were in the way. Eddie was forever hurdling rails and gutters and insulated wiring as he crossed to the opposite side.

A variety of noises and smells filled his senses with each passing step, but the dominant rumble came from an electrical generator, and the dominant odor was grease.

At last, Eddie arrived at the northernmost end where random-sized wood cabinets lined the entire wall, some as large as closets. On the door of each cabinet was the handwritten word "prototype" usually followed by a letter—or by a letter and a series of numbers—or by a letter, a series of numbers, and a title such as *Chronological Perception: Accelerator/Decelerator* or *Uniglottal Neurological Translator.* One cabinet had nothing written on. Its sides were thick metal and six padlocks insured its inaccessibility. From the thickness of dust on its surface, it appeared this particular cabinet hadn't been opened in decades. Eddie had the distinct impression these were inventions—a whole row of them—unpublished and unpublicized. What might a *Chronological Perception: Accelerator/Decelerator* be? His curiosity tugged against his better judgment. Reaching toward the cabinet where these words were etched, Eddie found the latch and lifted.

As the door opened, the shadow which hid the cabinet's contents fled. The object inside made Eddie cock an eyebrow and curl up one corner of his mouth. What the heck was it?

It looked like a life jacket, but it was too thin. It would formfit a wearer's entire torso down to the hips. Jutting out from the shoulders were two wire rods, like the cross support inside the arms of a scarecrow. At even intervals along the length of each rod were leather straps, apparently designed to fasten against a wearer's arms and wrists. At the tip of each rod were two small circular disks with dials sized to be finger controls.

What could it be used for? If there had been a motor on back, he'd have guessed it was a jet pack. If it contained anything mechanical or electrical, the circuits would be hidden under the layers of material. Eddie felt the jacket's mylar-smooth surface. He slipped his fingers under the base and lifted slightly to determine its weight. He'd first thought the jacket would be ultralight and flexible, but whatever was woven within the lining was unexpectedly heavy. His fingertips pressed the jacket's front over the area which might cover one's heart. There was something bulky here. As he reached closer to feel the inside layer for a sense of how the lumpy patch was shaped, someone spoke from a dim corridor at the other end of the wall.

"Hello, Edward. Thank you for coming."

• *FOUR* •

Upon hearing the voice, Eddie jerked away from the cabinet. His eyes fixed on the shadowy figure in the corridor. The man might have been there all along, watching Eddie's curious fingers pry into places they didn't belong. Eddie saw visions of police cars and handcuffs and youth detention halls.

"I didn't take anything! I swear!" Eddie defended.

"Relax," replied the voice from the shadow. "I know. You wouldn't be here at all if I hadn't invited you. I heard your knock upstairs, but you didn't give me time to answer."

The man's voice was slurred. There was something wrong with his tongue. It was especially obvious when he used letters like r, n, t, or l. When he said "Edward" it could have just as easily been "Ebwood."

Eddie squinted, trying to perceive the figure's face. He could only make out the shape of his head. It was an odd shape, strangely asymmetrical. If there was hair, it consisted of a few tufts on the right side. That was all Eddie could see. That, the wheelchair, and the slippers at the end of his lifeless legs. Eddie expected him to roll forward into the light. He almost feared it. But shyly, the man stayed put, knowing the shadow was his veil.

"Why did you . . . *invite* me?" asked Eddie.

"Because you wanted to be invited," the man replied. "And because I wanted to invite you. Both are crucial criteria.

More crucial than you know. Ah, Edward, how long I've been waiting for you to ask me this! For you the wait was only a day. For me, it's been a lifetime."

"Then it's true," Eddie concluded. "You sent me a signal. You *put* something in my brain!"

"It's not all that grisly. The signal is harmless. If you concentrate a moment, you'll notice it's also gone."

He was right. The urge which had haunted Eddie since Saturday night was missing from his mind. How did Louis do it? Or perhaps more importantly, *why* did he do it?

"Why not write me a letter? Or call me on the phone? Or even wave me over as I walked by your gate?"

"What if you hadn't come?" was his response.

It was an odd reply. "Why wouldn't I have?" Eddie further challenged.

The man didn't answer. Instead, he introduced himself. "I'm Louis Kosserinski. I tell you this not because you don't already know, but because there should be some sort of etiquette between us, don't you think?"

Eddie realized he was still trembling. To cover his fear, he curtly demanded, "What do you want? And why me?"

"We can help each other, Edward."

"Help each other do what?"

"Achieve peace of mind." Louis exhaled long and deep. It made a slight whistle.Eddie didn't like talking with a shadow. He took a bold step forward. "What do you need me to—?"

"NO!" Louis roared. "Don't come any closer!"

Eddie froze in his tracks. Louis's shriek sent lightning up his spine. Eddie had a flashback. Grandpa Paxton. The nursing home. A day when Grandpa lashed out at one of the nurses for refusing to salt his oatmeal.

Louis sobered his voice. "I'm afraid I'm not much to look at, Edward."

"I understand," Eddie replied.

Louis spoke again. "In answer to your question, I need many things. I'm old, boy. I can't control the elements of flesh and bone as I once could. In the past there were people who would help me. They're getting old, too. We're all getting much too old."

"What do you need?" Eddie coaxed.

"Ketchup . . . for starters," answered Louis. "I'm afraid I didn't plan for ketchup very well. None since February."

Eddie half-smiled. "I can handle that."

He found himself tempted to step forward again, but caught himself. *Why do I want to move closer? What perverted thing within me wants to see him outside that shadow?*

"Anything else?" Eddie asked.

"That will do for now, but . . . you must come back tomorrow."

"I don't know if I can," Eddie said. "I got school the next—"

"You must come back tomorrow!" he repeated. "Do you really think you're safe until then?"

"Safe?"

"Yes! From the ones who would hurt you?"

Eddie lightly touched a knuckle to his bruised eye. *How would he know about that?* Certainly he'd seen commotion outside the gate that night, but his view would have been too narrow. *There's no way he could know that the feud was unresolved.* "Yeah, I'm safe," Eddie answered. "I can take care of myself."

"Perhaps I can help you take care of yourself even better." Louis proclaimed.

"Oh yeah? How're you gonna do that?"

"The jacket."

Louis was referring to the object inside the cabinet marked *Chronological Perception: Accelerator/Decelerator*—the same strange outfit which Eddie's fingers had been exploring when he first heard Louis's voice.

"What's it do?" Eddie asked.

Louis evaded the question, but offered some instructions. "When you wear it, make sure that it's positioned tightly over your heart. That way it can become one with the organ's rhythm."

"Do those wire things produce death rays or something?" Eddie wasn't sure if he was joking or not. He swallowed while awaiting a reply.

"You'll discover what it does easily enough. If I explained

it to you now, you'd strut away laughing and tag me a crazy old man. Then I'd never see you again because you'd wonder if crazy old men might be dangerous."

Eddie turned and looked at the jacket. His arms reached out and lifted it off its wooden pegs. It really *was* heavy. Despite the thinness of padding and material, it nearly dragged him to his knees. The lining of the jacket's vest looked like a Los Angeles road map. Circuits were criscrossing everywhere. The circuits would sit directly against a wearer's body, uninsulated. Eddie wondered if it could be used as an execution device—one step up from an electric chair.

"This thing isn't gonna make my future kids come out with three heads, is it?" asked Eddie.

Louis laughed. Or was it a laugh? The sound was dreadful—more like choking. Eddie peered into the shadowy corridor until the noise ended. He vowed never to say anything else which Louis might interpret as a joke—not if he'd have to hear that horrible gurgle again.

"Don't wear the jacket with a shirt underneath," Louis continued. "It must be flush with your skin. After you've strapped the wire rods securely against your arms with the disks sitting snugly at the base of your palms, you may turn the knobs. Turn them inward, or turn them outward—simultaneously. But not too far! Too far inward and the jacket may freeze you. Too far outward and it may cook you alive."

Eddie started lifting the jacket back onto its wooden pegs. "M-Maybe you should keep this. I can find something else to protect me. A nice gun or something."

"Don't be foolish!" Louis scolded. "If you treat it with the utmost care and refrain from using it foolishly, the jacket is more harmless than a microwave. Take it. You'll quickly discover its applications. You'll never have to fear those boys again. You'll never have to fear *anyone* again. Fear is not an attribute of God, my young friend. It's a fever, like a plague, and often as fatal. No one should feel such diseased emotions. The truth is, I've allowed fear to persist in the world far too long. You, Edward Fanta, hold the vaccine. Administer it carefully. Very carefully."

Eddie squinted hard at the face in the shadow. *Is this guy on the same planet as I am?* Suddenly, he wanted to get out—get out now. Without further hesitation, he took the jacket. He moved to make a speedy exit, offering a quick, "Thank you."

"Tomorrow then?" Louis repeated.

"Sure. You bet," Eddie replied uncertainly and made his way toward the door.

Louis watched him hurdle the rails and gutters. He watched him escape up the ramp. He watched until the boy's shadow had disappeared behind him.

Louis closed his eyes. "It's begun."

*   *   *   *

Outside, with the jacket weighing down his arms, Eddie blew a sigh of relief. It was over. He was still alive. He felt silly for having trembled the way he did. He wouldn't tell Duck about the trembling.

Eddie was walking home on clouds. He was the only kid alive who could claim an actual conversation with the legendary Lizard Man.

And then there was the jacket.

By the time Eddie arrived at his apartment, the jacket's weight was causing sweat to appear on his brow. He'd wanted to hop over to Duck's side of the duplex and tell him all about the confrontation. But Eddie's imagination was bubbling. He had to discover what the jacket could do.

His mother's car was parked up the street at the home of one of her neighborhood friends, another single mother with comparable sob stories. Eddie entered the house and rushed the jacket into his bedroom, where he laid it carefully upon his comforter.

After securing the deadbolt, he grabbed the chair from his desk and positioned it before his bed. He stripped off his shirt, tossing it in the corner where it caught on the lamp and hung. Then Eddie Fanta sat gawking at his strange toy.

He'd never felt such anticipation—not even the night he'd waited for Tanya outside the Valley Fair Movies Nine. He thought about the official title Louis had etched on the cabinet where the jacket was housed. "Chronological" was defined easily enough. It had to do with time. Maybe this was a time machine! *An actual time machine!* "Perception" was also a simple word, but Eddie wasn't quite sure how it applied here. "Accelerator/ Decelerator" were easy terms. But when Eddie tried to make sense of the entire phrase together, he came up blank.

Eddie wriggled his fingers like a mad scientist. He hoisted the jacket over his right shoulder and then over his left. After tightening the straps at his waist and under his armpit, he wrapped the leather bands carefully around the length of each arm. The metal rods were more flexible against his limbs than he'd first imagined; he bent them with his elbows effortlessly. Having tightened the last band on his right wrist, Eddie settled back in his seat. He placed his elbows on his knees, his fingers extended. Under each palm sat the knobby disks. *Turn simultaneously inward or outward:* Those were Louis's instructions. His thumb and index finger pinched both knobs.

Eddie Fanta closed his eyes, held his breath, and turned inward.

Gulp! Eddie wished perhaps he hadn't held his breath. The jacket sucked in and around his torso. Every pocket of air between his skin and the jacket's lining hissed out around his neck. Eddie grew claustrophobic, terrified of becoming akin to a python's meal. Then he realized the jacket adjusted while he breathed, a perfect expansion and contraction to match the expansion and contraction of his lungs. The jacket seemed lighter, more formfitting than a wet suit. Except for the lumpy material over his heart and upper chest, he might even be able to wear a loose sweatshirt over the top with no one suspecting he had it on. In fact, the bulkiness of his chest might lead some to believe nature had made him superior to the average-built male.

Eddie turned the knobs a little farther inward.

Nothing was happening. He'd wondered if he might see the sun and the moon fly past his window or if he might see evidence of the changing seasons on the leaves of the trees, like in that old movie, *The Time Machine*. Everything was silent and still. The air in his room tasted stale.

Eddie gave the knobs a full two turns. Just as Louis had warned, Eddie felt cold. More than that, the farther he turned, the tighter the knobs became. But just as before, nothing much was changing.

"Riiight!" Eddie sarcastically crooned. "This thing'll sure show those Copperheads a thing or two."

Eddie snorted in disappointment. His dreams of visiting the 24th century to rub shoulders with Captain Jean-Luc Picard quickly dissipated. It *was* getting awfully chilly though, so Eddie turned the knobs back to the starting point.

A moment passed. A look of perplexity formed on Eddie's face. He furrowed his brow and sniffed. Something *was* different. The mustiness which had dominated the air only seconds before was gone. What had happened? Eddie couldn't put his finger on it, but his senses told him there *had* been a subtle change in the environment of his bedroom.

Eddie's fingers pinched the knobs a second time and turned. There it was again! That musty smell. Eddie surveyed the room. The light emanating from his lamps was different. Was it dimmer? No, that wasn't it.

Eddie glanced at the digital clock on his dresser. He seemed to remember the time had been 9:17 when he finished strapping the jacket onto his arms. Oddly, it was *still* 9:17. He'd have guessed it to be a few minutes later.

Eddie arose and moved toward the window.

That's what was different!

When he'd arrived home earlier, there was a definite breeze because he remembered how good it felt after sweating under the weight of the jacket. At present, not a single leaf on the tree above his window was jiggling. What was more, the world had gone silent!

Even from this distance, Eddie could usually hear the trucks on the interstate or children playing in neighboring yards. And where was the eternal clanking of the water heater outside his bedroom door? Eddie couldn't hear a thing. Had the jacket made him deaf?

No—wait. He heard something. A low hum seemed to float in the air and permeate everything. Eddie turned the knobs back again, this time very slowly. As he did, he fixed his vision on the tree branches outside his window. As his fingers turned, he began to sense movement. The leaves began fluttering. Eddie noticed a bird flying in his frame of vision. But the bird was moving so slowly Eddie thought at first it was a faraway jet against the fading blue sky. As the knob clicked back into its starting position, the bird whipped across the frame and out of sight. The leaves on the tree were dancing furiously as a gust of wind reached its climax and subsided. The water heater let out a clank.

And the digital clock flipped to 9:18.

Ohhh my gosh, Eddie uttered under his breath.

He turned the knobs inward a *third* time. The leaves danced slower and finally ceased moving.

I just stopped the world! I stopped everything!

Eddie twisted the knobs a quarter turn back and forth as rapidly as he could. The room began *pulsating—pulsating—pulsating*. His eyes sank backwards and forwards in their sockets. It wasn't the light which pulsated and it wasn't the air. If anything, it was gravity itself!

Eddie's stomach did a somersault. He clicked the knob back to start in time to heave the remains of his lunch on the carpet. Eddie dropped to all fours beside his bed.

Groaning deeply, he concluded, *This is no toy. Rapid turning is* out!

Eddie sat back against his door, wiped his mouth with the shirt hanging on the corner lamp, and then wiped the carpet. The nausea was gone. But his bewilderment intensified.

What would happen if I turned it the other way?

Ignoring his recollection of the nausea, Eddie's fingers pinched the knobs again, only this time he turned them slowly and simultaneously *outward*.

The minute display on his digital clock began flipping like

a pinwheel. The leaves were now vibrating so fast they resembled a hummingbird's wings. When Eddie had arrived home, the sky was only beginning to fade; but in a matter of seconds, as Eddie turned the knobs farther outward, the sky went instantly black, as if someone had shut off the sun with a light switch. When Eddie finally turned the knobs back to start, the digital clock read 10:41 and the heat left him wet with perspiration.

It is a time machine! Well, maybe not a time machine per se, but a . . . a . . . Chronological Perception: Accelerator/ Decelerator!

Wow! Eddie shouted in his mind.

"Double wow!" he shouted out loud.

Duck has to see this! Eddie sprang to his feet, and unlatched the deadbolt. The jacket felt light as a feather. He burst through the house and threw open the front door. A car's headlights were moving down the street. *The ultimate test!*

Eddie turned the jacket's knobs slowly inward. Sure enough, the car, which had been moving at thirty MPH, slowed down to a speed which wouldn't allow it to reach the end of the block for well over an hour by Eddie's perception. The noise from its engine slowed down as well, like some kind of Doppler reverberation.

Eddie laughed boldly. *I can do anything! Absolutely* anything*!*

He skipped across the lawn to the other side of the duplex, knocking *shave-and-a-haircut, two bits* onto Duck's front door.

He waited for awhile, then he realized the knobs were still twisted inward a quarter turn. The Hos might not answer the door for a very, *very* long time.

Eddie turned around. The station wagon in the street was still inching along—or should he say "centimetering" along. He trotted down the driveway and into the street where he could look right into the car's window. Eddie saw that the driver was a lady, pointing her finger at three preschool-aged children in back. Apparently, she was in the process of bawling them out. Their expressions were frozen in an attitude of forlornness. Eddie stood in front of the car, its headlights glaring into his face. His arms were akimbo, like

Superman before a powerful locomotive. He knew if he were to turn the knobs back to start at this instant, it would end his life—crush him under the station wagon's grill! *This is too much! Way, way too much!*

Eddie laughed again and danced back to Duck's front door. His knock still hadn't been answered. Eddie sighed. The sound of the knock might not have even registered in their ears yet! Eddie turned the knobs back to start. The station wagon sped away, having never even noticed the flash of his presence. After a few seconds, Duck answered the door with a look of alarm on his face.

"Eddie! It's *you!*"

"Of course it's me. Who did you expect?"

"What you do to our door?" Duck demanded. "It sound like machine-gun burst hit our door!"

Eddie clasped both of Duck's shoulders. His face was so wild with excitement that Duck tried to back away. Eddie's hold was firm.

"Duck. My friend. My Cambodian friend. My ultimate, *ultimate* friend!"

"What the matter with you, Eddie? Simmer down. My mother and sister trying to sleep." Duck glanced up and down his American pal. "Why you wear 'Man from Mars' suit?"

"Duck!" Eddie exclaimed. "*You and I can rule the world!*"

• *FIVE* •

Tonight Eddie Fanta decided there was a God . . . probably.

Strange I'd draw that conclusion, Eddie thought. Experiences like tonight would usually lead folks in the *opposite* direction, wondering if they *need* anything "Supreme." But Louis Kosserinski's jacket made Eddie feel nose to nose with the fabric of reality, exhilarated with the breath of life itself, convinced his existence could be no accident. God had arranged this entire universe, arranged everything he'd ever done, seen, or heard, strictly for *his* own benefit . . . or amusement. Eddie wasn't sure which yet.

Before his mother arrived home, Eddie dragged Duck into his living room to watch the jacket in action. With his friend perched on the sofa, Eddie spun both knobs carefully inward. To Lu-duc Ho's perception, Eddie Fanta became a blur. Then he disappeared entirely. Duck's eyes popped out like a jack-in-the-box. He was about to flee home in terror when Eddie reappeared again. Only now he was standing on the opposite side of the room.

"Holy Moses!" Duck screeched. To Duck, Eddie was only missing a couple seconds, but Eddie insisted three *minutes* had passed by his own perception.

"It's a *Chronological Perception: Accelerator/ Decelerator,*" Eddie authoritatively announced. "In other words, this baby speeds up or slows down our perception of time. Do you know what that means?"

Duck was still speechless. The urge to flee home hadn't fully subsided.

"It means," continued Eddie, "that whoever is wearing it can do anything he wants. *Anything*! If I wanted to see what was happening in the year 2022 A.D., I could see it. If I wanted to walk into a bank and take all the money in every register, I could do it! If I wanted to buy the *Utah Jazz* and increase Karl Malone's paycheck to one hundred million dollars a year, I could do it tomorrow!"

Eddie noted a pudgy, black fly buzzing across the living room.

"Watch that fly!" Eddie urged.

The insect was making its way to the kitchen when Eddie turned the knobs inward one-quarter turn. Eddie observed the insect stop in midflight—as frozen in space as one of the models dangling over his bed. Eddie stepped up to the fly and enclosed his palm around its body. He snatched it out of the air and glanced over at Duck.

His friend appeared equally frozen, his eyes still fixed on the spot Eddie had stood before. Eddie mischievously considered setting the fly loose in Duck's gaping mouth, but he suppressed the temptation. Instead, when he turned the knobs back to start, he reappeared directly before Duck's nose. The Cambodian's heart leaped into his throat. He jolted back against the cushions. When Eddie opened his fist, the fly was dead, apparently unable to make the transition. It dropped to the carpet. Duck watched it fall, still stupefied, his bronze complexion paler than Eddie had ever seen it.

"Are you okay, buddy?"

Duck replied with one uneasy nod.

Eddie continued his demonstration. "Now watch this!" Eddie turned the knob inward just a hair. To Duck's eyes, Eddie's hands, mouth, the wisps of his hair—all of it had the appearance of a movie in fast forward.

"If I barely turn the knobs this far," said Eddie, his voice like a cartoon chipmunk, "I could win every race I ever entered. Even the Olympics!"

"I not believe I see this," Duck muttered.

To Eddie, Duck's voice sounded like a record on the slowest speed. He turned the knobs back.

"Do you want to try it?" Eddie asked, his vocal chords normalized.

"No!" Duck answered abruptly. "You trying it just fine."

Eddie revealed to Duck all the details of his confrontation with Louis Kosserinski. Duck listened in awe, asking very few questions; and when Eddie was finished, the Cambodian promised he'd persuade his sister to drive them to the store in the morning for Louis's ketchup. Eddie's mother pulled into the driveway. Duck scooted home, his head still spinning. Eddie slipped into his bedroom. Later, his mother knocked on his door to check on him. Surprised to find it unbolted, she peeked in. Eddie was snuggled in his bed. The covers were pulled up over the jacket. She noticed Eddie's shirt curled up on the floor and the vomit stain on the carpet beside it. Instinctively, she rushed to Eddie's side to feel his forehead and cheeks.

"Are you feeling all right?"

Eddie hadn't been sick for so long, he couldn't remember the last time his mother had "mothered" him like this. The attention felt kinda good and it brought back nice thoughts.

"I'm fine. Something I ate didn't agree with me."

She reached down and picked up the shirt, wiping the stain a few times.

"I'll throw this in the wash. Can I get you anything?"

"No. I don't think so. I should be good-as-new in the morning. Don't worry."

His mother nodded and smiled warmly. Eddie thought he was looking at somebody else for a moment. Somebody ten years younger, without any lines. It seemed as though once-upon-a-time she always smiled like that.

She whispered, "Good night." As she turned away, Eddie stopped her.

"Mom," he called.

Her head poked back into the room. Eddie hesitated. He thought he might apologize again—this time in a way she'd believe was sincere. The words wouldn't come, so he settled with, "Thanks, Mom."

"You're welcome, Eddie." She closed the door.

*   *   *   *

Eddie tried to sleep. Truly, he did. He even took off the jacket and set it on the chair beside his bed. But his mind remained on full alert and he couldn't thin his adrenaline. Around 12:45 he gave up. *How can I be expected to sleep! I still have so much energy.*

Then it hit Eddie—*he didn't* have *to sleep!*

Eddie slipped the jacket back over his shoulders. He turned the knobs outward and watched the numbers on his digital clock start flipping at warp speeds. Over the next five minutes (or eight hours depending on who perceived it), Eddie experimented with the jacket's various velocities. He discovered that one full outward turn condensed an hour into a single second. This exhausted all the time he had for experiments because six full hours had flown by on the clock by the time he got it back to start. The sun had already risen.

The temperature within the jacket had become quite toasty. If he'd have turned the knobs much farther, the jacket might have left blisters on his skin.

So it really *wasn't* practical to think he could visit the distant future. Such a trip would doubtlessly leave his body in ashes. Still, the prospect of watching a couple days whip by while only a minute or so elapsed by his own internal clock was impressive enough.

The digital clock now read 8:36 A.M. His mother would already be up and off to work. Eddie shuddered to imagine what might have happened if his mother had checked in on him while he was in the heat of time travel. To her, Eddie would have appeared dead. There would have been no pulse; his eyes would have looked glassy and lifeless. The elapse of a few short seconds by Eddie's perception might have found him staring up at the ceiling of a dank drawer in the morgue! If the morticians were somehow able to remove the jacket before he could turn the knobs back to start, would that mean he was stuck in his decelerated reality forever? Best to use the fast-forward mode more discreetly in the future.

Eddie was famished. He ate three bowls of *Cocoa Crispies* and drank a glass of whole milk to wash it down. Three minutes later, he stood on Duck's doorstep while Duck's grumbling seventeen-year-old sister scoured the house for her car keys.

Eddie left the jacket under his bed. It was already eighty degrees and unless Eddie wanted to turn the knobs inward every few minutes for the benefit of its built-in air conditioning, it was too awkward to lug around.

They drove to Food-4-Less. Eddie and Duck located the ketchup while the sister checked out eyeliners. Eddie chose the most expensive brand. "After six months, Louis should have the best."

They moved the single bottles aside and took the whole case underneath. While dropping it into the shopping cart, Eddie noticed two boys with copper-topped haircuts at the end of the aisle.

He slipped behind Duck's shoulder, nearly knocking over a display of salad dressing. The two Copperheads took no notice and strutted on to the next aisle. Eddie handed Duck back his twenty dollar bill.

"Buy it for me," he pleaded. "I'll meet you in the car."

Duck agreed. Eddie crept back to the front of the store, past the cashiers, and into the parking lot. There were no more Copperheads outside. He laid low in the back seat of the car and kept an eye on the store entrance.

This is ridiculous. He couldn't hide from Mikey Swearingen and his posse forever. They'd catch him sooner or later. He wondered if Duck thought less of him for the way he reacted. *I hate this! How did I get caught up in this mess?*

The two Copperheads came out of the store before Duck and his sister had finished paying. They climbed into an old orange van down the way. Eddie recognized one of them—

the guy with the blood-red scalp whom Mikey had called Miguel. The other one may have been present that night as well. Eddie had been too frightened to memorize every face.

Miguel pulled a carton of *Marlboros* out from under his jacket. The other gangster, now in the passenger's side, was a more health conscious shoplifter. From one of his pockets he retrieved a nectarine. From another he pulled out a six-inch butterfly knife. Eddie watched him confidently flip the weapon into position and start excising the fruit from the pit. Miguel shut his door and revved up the engine.

Eddie crouched down as they sped away. If weapons such as that knife were standard issue in this gang, Eddie's fears might not be exaggerated. He'd use every means to avoid a confrontation. Who knew how accustomed Copperheads were to exercising such weapons? Today was the first time he'd ventured out of the neighborhood since Saturday night. He'd try to make it the last time he ventured away without Louis Kosserinski's jacket.

*   *   *   *

Duck's sister dropped Eddie off at Louis's gate. Duck was anxious to help him carry the case of ketchup inside, but Eddie advised against it.

"He's awfully shy," Eddie said. "I wouldn't want him thinking I considered him a freak show by bringing all my friends. Let me get him to trust me."

Eddie watched the car drive away. With his arms loaded down, he pushed through the gate and closed it with his shoulder. Recalling the cat, Eddie wandered around to the cellar. He entered unannounced, high-stepping across the rails and coolant gutters. He was determined to enter the corridor where Louis had been hidden. Somewhere in the back there had to be a stairway leading to the upper floor. That's where he'd finally knock.

Everything might have been fine—Eddie would have gotten no answer and gone back outside to knock on the front. But his forearms were starting to ache under the weight of the ketchup. He had to rest. After setting the case down on a crossing of rails, he shook the blood back into his elbows. Then he looked up.

Louis Kosserinski was sitting in a rail-drawn chair about twenty feet down the track. Only from this angle would Eddie have seen him. If the generator hadn't drowned out the sound of the boy's approach, Louis might have ridden around a nearby terminal, avoiding such an open display.

Perhaps it was best that it happened this soon. Eddie could no longer imagine things that weren't, or underestimate things that were.

Eddie's arms dropped to his sides. He became aware of his need to breathe. Because of that awareness, taking a breath felt unnatural, even uncomfortable. Most embarrassing of all, he could feel salty water gushing from his tear ducts. He tried to lift his lids wider so his eyes wouldn't overflow. *That's all this man needs*, Eddie thought. *Another sympathizer. Another mourner.*

Now Eddie knew why Louis hid, why he never went out in public. His person evoked a feeling of unbearable pity. How could any man bear knowing he inspired such vicarious suffering? Eddie also understood why so many legends had been created, why so much fear had been generated, and he couldn't help but wonder if the neighborhood children had actually been merciful. If a ten-year-old Eddie Fanta had caught a glimpse of this man, Eddie's legends would have caused far worse nightmares than any currently in circulation.

Louis wore thick glasses. An elastic band hugged them snugly around his head since he had no ear cartilage on which to hang the rims. So much was missing. So much displaced. So much held together with wire and pin. *That he's even alive!—that's the miracle! But how could living in such a form be any kind of miracle? My conclusion about the existence of God was a bit premature.*

Despite Eddie's efforts, a tear escaped his eye. He wiped it quickly with his shirt sleeve. Maybe Louis would interpret it as hay fever.

Louis was unmoving. The boy had seen him now. Louis's mind made an instinctive switch—a mental transformation of his physical condition. He could no longer be scarred and crippled. Now he was tall, his shoulders were broad, his features were flawless and regal. He sat in this rail-drawn cart only because it was comfortable. Louis edged the chair forward along the rail. As a result, Eddie could see every knot and causeway which made up Louis Kosserinski's scars as closely as the doctor who first unwound the bandages. In his right hand, badly disfigured above the knuckle, was a small plastic bottle of clear liquid which he used from time to time to moisten his eyes.

"Do you appreciate the jacket, Edward?" he asked.

Eddie understood why his words were slurred. Metal and elastic held his jaw together. Much of one cheek was torn away, making what was left of his tongue permanently chapped.

"Yes," Eddie shakily replied. "I appreciate it very much."

"Why aren't you wearing it?"

"I, uh—"

"You should always wear it. Without it, you're vulnerable to your enemies. It's not so heavy once you get used to it."

"You're right, it's not," said Eddie. With a final wipe, he absorbed the remaining water from his eyes. Embarrassed, he smiled. "All the chemicals down here. I must be allergic."

Louis nodded.

Eddie changed the subject quickly, "How did you do it? I mean, how did you build such a thing?"

"Einstein and Planck laid out most of the groundwork, took it right to the edge, but neither of them had the courage to jump. The unit does have its guardrails, as you might have discovered. A highway to the gods will always have guardrails. One can never go *too* far into the future. The heat becomes unbearable. Nevertheless, this Valentine's Day I should have lived seventy-five years. Yet in reality, I'm only sixty-eight. You can never totally *stop* time either. But you can stretch it—enough to live out your entire life while your friends are still locked inside puberty. It would be a cold life though—very cold."

Such knowledge coming from a man so void of human features. All those years watching *Star Trek*—all those alien life forms spewing forth superior intelligence—hadn't prepared Eddie's mind for this paradox.

"What other inventions do you have?" Eddie asked. "Do you have a jacket that takes you *back* in time as well?"

"No," he retorted. "Moving backwards in time is fundamentally impossible. Time can be stretched or compressed, but it can't be repeated. If it could, do you think I'd have let world history remain as it is? Do you think I'm that cruel?"

"No," Eddie hastily replied. His hopes of traveling back to prevent his family's dissolution popped like a soap bubble. Louis's mood was so volatile. Again, the crippled old man reminded him of his grandfather after the stroke.

"But I *do* have other inventions," Louis admitted, his voice now calmer. "I look forward to showing you more, when you're prepared. But not before."

Eddie perked up. "I can get prepared. I'll help you in any way I can. If it's running errands or fixing things or mowing your lawn, I'm your boy."

Louis appeared to have drifted far away for a moment. Eddie noticed Louis's eyes, dark brown and exceptionally clear. Enlarged by the lenses, they were his only feature left unscarred. But as Louis's thick glasses attested, even they were growing dim.

"My boy," Louis repeated to himself. He seemed to approve of Eddie's word choice. His attention fixed back on Eddie. A portion of scar tissue at Louis's cheek curled up. Eddie guessed this adjustment represented a smile.

"Thank you, Edward," said Louis.

*   *   *   *

For the next hour Eddie swept the old man's front sidewalk and searched the lawn for debris which might damage a mower. The boy's mind was still dominated by images of the old man's twisted features. Only a few minutes had elapsed. The images seemed more frightening than sad.

Eddie struggled against the fear. The agony Louis must have endured and must still be enduring. For the first time, Eddie was grateful for his meager blessings. And yet, he felt so selfish for thinking it that his gratitude brought him no comfort. Shortly after he'd starting making headway, Eddie became too exhausted to continue. His previous day had never really ended. It was as if he'd stayed up until four in the morning. The boy ambled to Louis's front door to apologize. As he knocked on the inner door, the killer feline emerged from one of the monitor shells. Eddie propped his back defensively against the wall. How could he have forgotten? But to his surprise, the cat was . . . purring?

With its tail undulating blissfully, the feline found Eddie's pant leg. While gliding against it, the animal released a rapturous "meow." Eddie remained as stiff as a post, not yet convinced this rattlesnake wasn't preparing to strike. He cautiously lowered his hand to pet its furry head. The cat poised its neck to meet his fingers and amplified its purr.

I definitely need to ask what invention made that *happen!*

When Louis came to the door, he was wearing a red sweatshirt with a hood to soften his appearance.

"I've gotta go," Eddie explained. "I promise I'll come back after school tomorrow."

"I want to show you something," Louis insisted.

Without waiting for Eddie's consent, Louis led the way through his kitchen. Eddie dragged his feet. He glanced at the kitchen cabinets. The drawers pulled down like periscopes, allowing Louis to obtain foodstuffs from the spaces within and push the drawer up again. Louis rolled past the cabinets and into the neighboring room. It was a study. Shelves climbed all the way to the ceiling; so many books it might have qualified as a school library. Louis wheeled over to a low center space in one of the shelves. There were no books in the space. On it was a row of tiny white knick-knacks.

"These are my animals."

Eddie moved closer. His mouth dropped in awe. They were animals all right—paper folded animals. A horse and a giraffe. A wolf and a peacock. A lion and an alligator. The craftsmanship was exquisite, just like . . .

Delicately, Eddie lifted the horse and balanced it on his palm. "They're beautiful," he whispered.

Louis watched the boy carefully. "It's a hobby," he said. "I've made so many, I can do it blindfolded. I thought you might like to see."

The boy looked up at the crippled old man. Could it be him? Could it actually be Grandpa Paxton behind those scars? It could be anybody! *No,* Eddie recalled. *I saw his body in the casket.* Again, the boy's eyes filled with tears. He was so tired now, anything might have brought his emotions to the surface.

Slowly, Louis nodded. *He's hooked.*

"I want you to read to me."

Eddie could barely keep his eyes open as it was, yet he found himself agreeing. "Sure. What?"

"A chapter of God's word. It's been so long. My eyes have grown dim." Louis handed Eddie a large-type three-in-one of the *Book of Mormon,* the *Doctrine and Covenants,* and the *Pearl of Great Price.* The boy slumped down in the billowing wing recliner at the center of the room. Louis wheeled around to face him.

"From the beginning?"

"Starting tomorrow," Louis replied. "Today I want you to read me the 'Olive Leaf'—*plucked from the Tree of Paradise, the Lord's message of peace* . . . Do you know the one I mean?"

"Sorry, I don't," Eddie admitted.

"Section 88. Are you a Latter-day Saint, Edward?"

"You bet. Through and through."

Eddie later wondered why he lied and couldn't come up with an answer. Louis knew he was lying anyway, especially when he had to ask twice which book Section 88 was in.

As he read, Louis seemed to drift into a trance. Eddie wasn't sure he was even listening, except his mouth moved from time to time. He recited many verses right along with the reading, as if half the book had been committed to memory.

The boy only made it to the forty-fourth verse which spoke

of the courses of the heavens and the earth: *"And they give light to each other in their times and in their seasons, in their minutes, in their hours, in their days, in their weeks, in their months, in their years—all these are but one year with God, but not with man."*

Eddie's voice faltered and faded. The book dropped to the recliner's arm and the boy's mind drifted into a world of dreams without having comprehended the substance of that final verse.

Louis comprehended though. He remembered the ideas which percolated in his mind when he'd once read those words long ago. Seeing Eddie asleep in the recliner, Louis covered the boy's lap with a blanket. Then he rolled his wheelchair back a pace and watched Eddie's face. He lifted his scarred hand, tempted to tousle the boy's hair, as he'd often done to his own son decades back. It had been so long since he'd touched human flesh. But this was not his son. He lowered his hand.

He was a bright boy, though. Exceptionally bright.

Here, at last, sleeps the Gabriel of the new world. A world without fear. A world without ignorance. A world of which God will approve.

Something quaked inside Louis. He suppressed the feeling immediately. Had he really once been committed to concealing his genius from the world? Hide his candle under a bushel? Utter foolishness!

He felt the quake again. *Yes,* he admitted. There were still parts of his work which would always remain hidden. Parts like the *Harmonizer*. Such inventions would remain hidden forever.

Sighing long and deep, Louis wheeled his chair toward the hallway at the other end of the study. He beamed his misshapen smile at the cat, curled up in its paisley napping cave in the corner, and wheeled toward a room at the end of the hall where he would toil on his latest and probably his last, creation.

• *SIX* •

The following day, Jordan View High School was back in business. Bells were ringing, halls were bustling. Eddie Fanta felt like an alien being. Not just because of new school disorientation, but because of a rather odd jacket under his oversized University of Utah sweatshirt.

There was a huge "Welcome Back" assembly in the gym that first day. The theme of the assembly, as displayed on several banners strung from bleacher to bleacher, was "We're Here to PUMP YOU UP!" *a la* Arnold Schwarzenegger as satirized by *Saturday Night Live*. The main attractions were the *Falcons*, Jordan View's football heroes, and the *Falconettes*, Jordan View's pom-pom wavers. Speeches were presented by the principal, student body president, and representatives from most of the auxiliary organizations. There was much cheering, applauding, and heckling—enough hoopla to hold anyone's attention. As for Eddie Fanta, seated beside Duck amidst an enthusiastic cluster of sophomores, his attention was fixed on a brood of twenty to thirty copper-topped gangsters, male and female, seated at the upper left corner of the opposite bleacher. Some had their entire scalps dyed red, like Miguel. Others had dyed only a lock over their ears or a tail in back. A few even had stripes like a skunk.

Several teachers had tried to break up the Copperheads before the assembly began—make them sit in different areas of the gym so they couldn't incite a disturbance. They'd managed to congregate back together again. The school spirit exhibited in that corner of the auditorium was predictably mild. Then Mikey Swearingen stood to hail the cheerleaders. All male Copperheads joined in the salute, swinging their fists at the air in rhythm with a wolfish chant which shook the building.

Eddie also noticed that nestled among them was Tanya.

My emerald-eyed Tanya!

For the first time today, Eddie turned the jacket knobs inward. The cheers of the crowd sank to a low-pitched hum. The cheerleaders froze in mid-kick. The jacket's lining chilled, which actually felt great since wearing this outfit was making Eddie sweat like a farm animal. He climbed down from his place in the bleachers, accidentally bumping a fellow sophomore, and made his way to the center court of the gym. Eddie was the only soul in sight who wasn't photograph still.

Tanya was seated a third of the way up the opposite bleachers, between two of her girlfriends. Mikey Swearingen, too proud to be seen with a girlfriend on such an occasion, had posted himself at the very top. Tanya cheered with the rest, her mouth curved into a lipstick-ad smile, her blonde hair floating over her shoulders, her hands pressed together at the end of a clap.

Though Eddie knew she'd humiliated him to the marrow, though he was convinced she found him about as enticing as an iguana, and though he knew an association with her might lead to the shattering of every bone in his body, he still couldn't free himself from her spell. She'd given him his first real kiss. And what a kiss it had been! *You can't kiss like that without feeling some shred of . . . something. It just isn't possible!*

Eddie had to speak with her. He had to see the reaction in those lustrous green eyes when she saw him again. *Maybe she'd been threatened to divulge our date plans to the Copperheads. Maybe Mikey had hurt her. Oh,* Eddie seethed inside, *if he did . . .*

Watching Tanya's motionless eyes left Eddie slightly hypnotized. He leaned forward and lightly, tenderly, returned the kiss she'd given him at Raging Waters. When he pulled back, her expression was unchanged. Eddie knew it was because of the jacket. Still, it was disappointing not to have affected her even half as dramatically as she'd affected him. He returned to his place in the bleachers, twisting the knobs back to normal.

Duck was glaring at him when he returned. He'd seen something about Eddie's position change, like a jump-cut in a movie reel. Fortunately, Duck appeared to be the only one who noticed.

Eddie happened to glance at the fellow sophomore a few bleachers below whose hip he'd accidentally bumped. The boy was writhing in agony! Bewildered friends on either side were begging to know what was the matter. He lifted his shirt and revealed a rosy new bruise the size of an apple.

Eddie felt terrible! He had no idea such a casual bump while accelerated could cause so much damage. Yet when he thought about it, anything coming at a person a thousand miles an hour, even barely grazing them, would displace so much air it was bound to be quite painful.

Then it occurred to him: *Oh no! The kiss!*

Eddie arose and spotted Tanya across the auditorium. She was awkwardly climbing down the bleachers with the help of her two friends. Both of Tanya's hands were cupped over her mouth. She was leaving the assembly.

Eddie fought his way down through the crowd.

"Where you going?" Duck called after him.

Tanya exited through the north doors. Eddie exited through the south doors to head her off. Mikey Swearingen didn't think much of it when Tanya called out in torment and got up to leave, but his eye spotted Eddie Fanta almost the moment he stepped onto the gym floor. He gestured to a few of his minions and prepared to follow him.

When Eddie burst into the hallway, Tanya and her friends were moving swiftly in his direction. Her friends were insisting she tell them how it happened. With her hands still shrouding her mouth, she replied through a choke of tears, "I have no idea. It's like my lips just exploded!"

Tanya's words filled Eddie with dread.

"Tanya!" he cried. Stepping in front of her, he yanked her hand away from her face. He was relieved. Tanya had exaggerated. Her lips weren't even bleeding, but they were beet-red and swollen. Her lipstick was smeared. Tears had made her eye makeup run. How horrifying if he'd kissed *her* the way she'd kissed *him*. It might have been the kiss of death!

"I'm so sorry," Eddie whimpered.

Tanya was stunned. How could anyone be so boorish? She gave Eddie a lethal glare. She noticed a smudge of lipstick on Eddie's upper lip—*oddly it was her color!*

Tanya pulled away, "Get out of my way you little creep!"

She concealed her mouth again and continued down the hallway toward the nurse's office. Her friends glanced back at Eddie, suggesting he was the rudest creature on the planet.

Five fingers pushed hard into the small of Eddie's back. He staggered forward a step, then turned around to face Mikey Swearingen and three of his cohorts.

"What do you think you're doin'?" Mikey demanded.

His fingers still projected like daggers, the Copperhead thrust them toward Eddie's chest, pushing him toward the wall. But Mikey recoiled in pain, shrieking a profanity. The tips of his fingers hadn't been prepared for the jacket's metal breastplate.

"What's under that shirt?!"

A faculty member arrived to break up the ruckus. She threatened everyone to get back to the assembly or follow her to the vice principal's office.

"But I want to see what's the matter with my girlfriend!" Mikey whined, theatrically.

The lady showed no sympathy and repeated her threat. Mikey and his fellow Copperheads strutted back toward the gym's north doors. As Eddie was about to reenter the south doors, Mikey called over to him. Eddie stopped. The Copperhead leader waited until he was certain Eddie was watching, then he made his hands into fists and smashed them together out in front of his chest. Finally, he twisted them against one another as if violently wringing an imaginary newspaper. Symbolically, the gesture represented wringing the head off a snake. Anyone who knew the hand signals of the Copperheads knew this sign was the worst possible threat a person could receive. Coming from the leader himself, it wasn't a good omen at all.

High school wasn't turning out to be as enjoyable as Eddie had hoped.

*   *   *   *

"I almost killed her, Duck," Eddie ranted. Duck was lying back on Eddie's bed, growing dizzy watching his friend pace back and forth. The infamous jacket hung over the chair.

"As it is," Eddie continued, "it's like I punched her in the mouth."

"She deserve it for standing you up that night," commented Duck.

"No," Eddie countered. "You don't understand. I *love* her, Duck."

The Cambodian groaned, "She hate *you*, Eddie. She treat you like day-old fish guts. You give this up or I make appointment for you with school psychiatrist."

Eddie indicated the jacket. "I've got to be more careful with that thing. It's *dangerous!*"

"Sounds like just the weapon you need to fight Copperheads."

Eddie faced Duck to be sure he was listening. "Don't you get it? If I were to punch Mikey Swearingen while I was accelerated, I'd bash his brains in!"

"Better him than you. He give you 'twisted snake.' That mean you have to watch your back every minute—maybe for rest of your life."

Eddie continued pacing, "I've got to find some way to scare him. Some way to intimidate him so badly he and his Copperhead bootlickers will never bother me again."

"Why not you hit them where it hurt most. Speed yourself up and shave their heads. Or even better, dye their hair gross color!"

"That's a good start, but there's one major problem. Anything I touch while the knobs are turned inward is practically destroyed. If I barely set my finger on a tube of toothpaste, the stuff shoots across the room, at *both* ends, like it was exploding out of a fire hose. The other night I nearly tore my bedroom door off its hinges. I picked up my model of the *Batmobile,* and it shattered in a million pieces. I even need to be careful where I step. Walking on the second story of some flimsy building might send it crashing to the ground! Remember how I killed that fly? All I did, Duck, was cup it in my hands."

"You say Louis Kosserinski just give you this thing?"

Eddie thought a moment. "Maybe he doesn't fully understand his own invention. After all, the man never leaves his own house. He might've never put himself in a position to know its full ramifications."

"Or maybe, like Brother Fayle say, he not playing with full deck anymore. Maybe he not even *care* that you might hurt somebody. Maybe he not even know the difference. I advise you stay away from him."

Eddie resented Duck's statement. "He's a crippled old man! You think I should just leave him to rot?"

Duck backed off. "Sorry! Just suggestion!"

After his friend had gone home, Eddie lay back on his bed and wondered why he'd gotten so upset. He found himself drifting off to memories of his grandfather. Louis Kosserinski had sparked something inside him. Something he missed terribly. Helping this old man was a kind of penance. It seemed to ease an inner pain which had never quite healed. Eddie returned to Louis's house that night. He read him another chapter from the *Book of Mormon.* When he was finished, he described for Louis the problem he and Duck had discussed about being unable to use or touch anything while accelerated.

Louis responded brazenly. "Where are your God-given powers of deduction, Edward? Why do you think your clothing doesn't fall apart? Why do you think the dirt under your nails remains intact?"

Eddie wanted another hint. He shook his head. "I'm not sure."

"To take something with you when you accelerate, it must be in your hand or on your person as you turn the knobs—*it must be touching your skin!* Use your mind, boy! I won't be here to inspire you forever."

Eddie's eyes lit up with understanding.

Operation Anti-Copperhead was coming together quite nicely.

*   *   *   *

Mikey Swearingen waited patiently inside the pocket.

The pocket was an old entrance to Jordan View's football stadium, a high chain-link fence with interwoven wooden strips on either side of a short chain-link gate. The entrance fell into disuse when they expanded the stadium a few years back. The outdoor bleachers now came right up to the fence, making the view over the gate akin to looking into a triangular cave with hundreds of crisscrossing supports. Maintenance people used the entrance now and then to get under the bleachers and clean up the paper cups and popcorn boxes which patrons dropped under their seats. Otherwise, a padlock and chain tied it shut. During football games, the faculty usually placed a security man there to prevent kids from sneaking in without paying. But this afternoon, the field was empty. The padlock had been clipped with a huge pair of wire cutters shortly after final period let out.

Today is the day, Mikey chanted to himself. For a month he'd been waiting, watching, sniffing the air for an opportunity to strike. Mikey was the first to admit that his vendetta against Eddie Fanta was a watery one. It wasn't as if the kid had stolen some "powder" or wasted a brother. The nitty gritty of it was that the little punk had insulted him. Made him look bad in front of the crew. *Three punches! This could have all been over!* Mikey was truly annoyed. He had much more important things to do with his time. If it'd been just between him and Eddie that night, he'd have shrugged off this whole affair weeks ago. But the crew had seen it. Miguel had seen it. Maintaining leadership as one of a handful of Anglos in a predominantly Hispanic gang wasn't an easy task. The natives were getting restless. He'd been called out twice already this year. The second challenger still had both his arms in casts. "I fell down the stairs," he'd told the nurse. Mikey chuckled at the memory and pulled another drag off his Marlboro.

The fact was, he'd twisted the snake at this boy. Granted, he was overcome with a rush of temper at the time, but it was too late to take it back now. If you "twist the snake" at someone, tradition demands that individual has to go down hard. Death in some cases. In every case, it had to be something the receiver would never forget—a facial scar, a severed ear. In Eddie Fanta's case, Mikey opted to break his leg backwards, right at the knee joint. *Let him think about me every time he limps.*

Mikey had put a lot of thought into how he could turn this thing to his advantage without it being a waste of time. The talk in the air suggested that if Mikey was willing to cripple a kid simply for insulting him, he was one bad hombre. It might keep the wolves off his back for a long time, might earn him respect in circles he'd never considered.

He needed something new. Old rumors about wasting a couple guys in California were wearing off. Besides, as far as Mikey was concerned, he'd never killed *anybody.* That West Hollywood dude with the big mouth smoked the stuff on his own accord. Mikey just conveniently forgot to tell him it was bad. And that other one was strictly self-defense. *He came at me with a knife!* It didn't matter that the kid was only twelve. *Twelve years old or no twelve years old, I got a right to react.* To avoid the heat of that incident, Mikey moved to Salt Lake City to live with his older brother. He'd orchestrated two drive-bys since moving to this town—both Asian trash—but he wasn't the trigger man. That was Miguel. And besides, both those slant-eyes lived. They'd reportedly given up gang banging though, turned in their colors, which was all Mikey wanted in the first place.

To Mikey Swearingen, people were an orchestra and he played them like Bernstein. He couldn't afford to be a shooter at this point in his career. Connections in L.A. were starting to put a lot of trust in him. The day would come when he'd have to turn in his high-profile look and don a suit jacket and tie. Until then, he had to play it cool. Even school was important. Whereas other crack-pushing gangs were playing hooky ninety-nine percent of the time, Mikey pushed himself and his fellow gangsters to maintain a "C" average. Reactions to this policy were side-splitting. Some teachers even looked to him as a kind of leather-clad Lone Ranger. Mikey was certain that after age thirty, the human brain had atrophied to a state of total gullibility.

Mikey was looking to the day when not so much as an aspirin could get in and out of Salt Lake County without his approval. After all, a man's gotta have goals. To meet those kind of goals, a lot of folks have to trust you. Especially the *choias*—the police. To accomplish this, Mikey resorted to political narking, which meant he turned in a few street pushers now and then. Strictly low-level scum and almost always from rival gangs. *Political* narking was okay. It was all part of free enterprise—eliminating the competition. The narcotics division even gave him a code name for anonymity. *Snow Ranger.* The name cracked Mikey up.

Once Mikey had to turn in one of his own, a move which earned him the cop shop's undying devotions. See, most policemen were over thirty. Mikey wondered if he'd have to take out Miguel the same way one day. Miguel was hard-core, but he was too much of a hothead to run a serious gang. Mikey couldn't afford to let Miguel's rashness end up flushing his growing empire down the toilet.

Miguel was kneeling in the shadows about ten feet away, listening to Charmer recite a joke, one so crude the punch line didn't really matter. Mikey shook his head and lit another cigarette. *So childish. So fourth grade. How did I get hooked up with some of these guys?*

Salt Lake, Mikey mused. *Boy, this town sure produces some lunkheads.* Some gangs were so unsophisticated, they'd paint a wall with slogans in another gang's colors! In L.A. if you walked into some neighborhoods with even so much as the wrong colored shoelaces, you might walk out with broken ribs. *They're learning*, Mikey thought confidently. *I just gotta keep on 'em.*

It was starting to get dark. Mikey was beginning to wonder where Eddie Fanta was. For the last two nights, Eddie had been staying after school, trying out for a play—the *Sound of Music*. Mikey shoulda figured the little wimp would be into "*theat-ah.*"

When a fellow gangster reported that Eddie's name was posted on the final callback list, he knew the opportunity was too perfect to pass up. To get to the bus stop, Eddie had to walk down the very sidewalk which ran beside the pocket. Most of the other aspiring actors, including the drama teacher, would almost certainly exit by the main doors on the opposite side to the parking lot. Mikey's only worry was whether some jerk might offer Eddie a ride home. However, according to sources, that hadn't happened the two previous nights.

At last, the theater's rear door flew open and out stepped Eddie Fanta. It was too good to be true—the little maggot was alone.

"Miguel," Mikey whispered, drawing his henchman's attention to Eddie's approach.

Miguel had volunteered to grab him around the neck and drag him under the bleachers where they could perform their operation in privacy.

Other gang members informed each other of Eddie's appearance. Mikey hissed at them to shut up, then he crouched down where he could see the approaching boy through a slit in the fence.

In the silence, Mikey smiled. Eddie was wearing yet another sweatshirt. The guy seemed to have a million of them. No doubt, underneath he was still sporting that bullet-proof vest of sorts which Mikey's fingertips had encountered a few weeks before. The fact that he wore it every day was a piece of trivia now known to most of the school. *Too bad it never occurred to the punk that a shooter isn't the only way to mess up a guy.*

As Eddie drew closer, Miguel shifted into position. He had to remain hidden just left of the gate until the last moment. Eddie was so close now they could hear him whistling "Climb Every Mountain." Miguel felt a surge of adrenaline. He loved this. He loved this so much.

As Eddie passed in front of the pocket, Miguel tossed back the gate and sprang into action. Poor Mr. Fanta didn't even have the time to turn around to see his attacker before Miguel threw one arm around his neck and the other over the boy's mouth.

Then Eddie Fanta disappeared.

Miguel stood perfectly still for a moment, his arms remaining in their outstretched position, but the person he'd been pinning there only seconds before was one-hundred percent *gone*. Miguel's forearm and hand were bruised and sore—for no reason whatsoever!

"What happened!" cried Mikey, emerging from the shadows. "Where's he at?"

Miguel stuttered, "I-I-I had him, Mikey. I swear, I-I had him."

The other Copperheads emerged from the pocket with their heads scoping every direction for a sign of Eddie Fanta.

"What do you *mean* you had him?! *Tell me where he went!*" Mikey demanded.

But Miguel's attention was aimed at the sidewalk. There was a message etched there with bright red chalk: *Mikey Swearingen—leave Eddie Fanta alone OR DIE.*

"Who wrote that?" yelled Mikey. "Was it there before?"

The other gangsters were shaking their heads, "I don't think so, man."

Everyone's eyes turned on Charmer. His buzz top was no longer copper-colored. The predominating hues were now yellow and orange. Charmer was massaging his scalp with both hands. The top of his head felt raw and irritated all of a sudden. When he noted that everyone was gaping at him, he looked at his hands and saw the wet yellow-orange dye. Charmer belted out a profanity.

And then Eddie's voice silenced everyone.

"Is the message clear?"

They turned. Eddie Fanta stood a few yards away.

"Touch me again," he threatened, "and I'll haunt every one of you—even in your dreams!"

Mikey'd had enough of this. Jaw clenched and fists cocked, he launched into Eddie. But each time he swung, Eddie jumped out of the way. His speed was astounding! Mikey had never seen anything like it! During Mikey's final, most desperate lunge, Eddie vanished again. Mikey tripped into his own swing, tumbling onto the cement.

Several Copperheads were already fleeing into the school. Mikey's main henchmen, Miguel and Torrence, were all who remained when Mikey suggested they make a mad dash for the car.

They ran around the side of the building. Every twenty feet they passed another chalk-drawn message on the school's bricks: *This is a warning! Leave Eddie Fanta alone! If you want to live, don't bother Eddie Fanta!*

When they finally arrived at Mikey's Buick, the hood was dripping gold paint. It read: *Are you getting the message yet, Mikey?*

"My car!" Mikey yelled. "The maggot ruined it!"

"Who cares?" cried Miguel. "Let's get outta here!"

The three Copperheads dove into the Buick. Mikey turned the ignition and the car lurched into the street. He pushed the Buick to sixty miles per hour though it was only a twenty-five zone. No one seemed to object.

A few blocks later, as they were turning down Redwood Road, another message blazed across the windshield, leaving a crack from one end of the glass to the other. Mikey started fishtailing, narrowly avoiding a Volvo in the other lane. This new message read: *Have I made myself clear, Mikey?*

Mikey jammed on the brakes before running a light at a busy intersection. Miguel and Torrence used this opportunity to escape.

"Where are you going?" Mikey called after them.

"Sorry, Mikey," cried Miguel, slamming the door. "Sounds like this is your problem, *Amigo*."

Mikey spewed profanities after them. They were already a half block away. The light turned green and Mikey punched the accelerator, breathing threats against Eddie Fanta under his breath.

"What's that you're saying?"

Mikey turned to see a new passenger seated beside him.

"Aren't we squared away on this Eddie Fanta thing yet?" Eddie deadpanned.

Mikey replaced his look of fury with horror. As suddenly as the figure of Eddie Fanta had appeared in the passenger's seat, it disappeared again. The instant it left, the passenger door to the Buick dropped off its hinges and bounced into the street. Several drivers behind the Buick honked as they swerved to avoid the debris.

Mikey didn't consider going back for the door. He sped toward his brother's house. The sweat streaming off his forehead was stinging his eyes. As his vehicle approached an underpass, Mikey looked up to see a wide banner stretched as long as the lane. It read: *Well, Mikey, what do you say?*

Mikey zoomed under the banner. He turned right at the next corner, then took another right, and then a left. Each time he turned, the tires squealed, kicking up everything in their path.

He pulled into his brother's driveway. The Buick skidded to a stop. Mikey leaned forward against his steering wheel, hyperventilating.

Safe, he thought—or rather, he hoped.

It was only after Mikey had closed and locked the front door behind him that he could finally *believe* this nightmare was over. His brother's wife was sitting on the sofa, trying to nurse a crying baby.

"What's the matter with you?" she inquired distastefully.

"Nothing," Mikey replied and strode back to his bedroom.

Finding his bed, Mikey pushed his dirty laundry onto the floor. He lay back, closed his eyes, and waited for his breathing to normalize. Grabbing a grimy T-shirt off the bedpost, he dabbed the sweat off his face.

It's over, he sighed. *It's really over.*

But his sweat continued to flow and drip with no hint of letting up. Mikey stepped across the hallway into the bathroom, locking the door behind him. For the most part, his breathing was stable. He opted not to think about what had happened. If he thought about it too long, he'd wonder if his mind had finally gone, just like his father had told him it would.

He looked at his face in the mirror while soaking a washcloth in the cool tap water. The rag felt refreshing. Mikey draped it over his head and bit the corner, sucking a few drops down his parched throat. As he began using it to wipe the back of his neck, he noticed another message, etched on the mirror with ruby-red lipstick: *So are you gonna leave Eddie Fanta alone or not?*

Mikey fell back against the towel rack, ripping its screws out of the wall. "Yes!" Mikey shrieked. "I'll leave him alone!"

Looking back at the mirror, Mikey saw that the message had changed. Lying beside the sink was one of the towels which had formerly hung on the rack. The lipstick from the previous message was smeared all over it.

The new message read: *I didn't hear you say "Scout's honor."*

"Scout's honor!" Mikey cried. He raised his arm to the square, but the sign his fingers made looked more like a Vulcan greeting. "Any honor you want!" Mikey Swearingen broke into tears.

The message changed again before Mikey's eyes, this time leaving a web of cracks in the mirror: *Thank you.* Then it changed again, leaving even more cracks: *And by the way, I owe you this.*

Eddie Fanta carefully slid his finger around the skin of Mikey Swearingen's eye, knowing that in his accelerated state it would leave a perfect raccoon-shaped shiner. Afterwards, Eddie opened the bathroom door, stepped out, closed it, and made sure it was locked (though if he had to, he could easily break in again with his toothpick). Eddie exited the house, skipped a block toward his home, and spun the knobs back to start.

Back inside his brother's house, Mikey watched the bathroom door drop off its hinges, falling clumsily against the opposite wall. Mikey's sister-in-law appeared in the doorway, enraged by the damage.

"You're gonna pay for this, Mikey! Every penny!"

Mikey, his eye swollen and pulsing, was slumped down on the floor. He looked up at his sister-in-law with a drained, witless expression, like a horse-whipped hound dog.

• *SEVEN* •

"*Rolf Gruber!*" exclaimed Eddie. "Who the heck is *Rolf Gruber?*"

As soon as Eddie arrived at school, he led Duck just short of an all-out run to the other end of the building, where the final cast list was posted on the drama room door. He'd been anticipating, hoping, *praying* he might follow the dotted line across the poster to find his name coupled with the character of Captain Georg von Trapp or Maximilian Detweiler—at least those were the parts Mr. Kasznar, the director, had called him back to read for. Instead, Eddie's eyes followed down, and down, and still *further* down the list of characters until he'd matched up his name with that of one, Rolf Gruber.

"He the messenger boy in love with the oldest girl," Duck confirmed. Duck was the resident expert on movie musicals. He fell in love with *Oliver!* when he was eight, though at the time, he could barely utter a word of English. *The Sound of Music* ran a close second in his list of favorites.

"A messenger boy! I sing my guts out for two weeks, memorize two audition scenes, endure two nights of callbacks—and Mr. Kasznar has the nerve to cast me as a *messenger boy?*"

"Be grateful," observed the upperclassman at Eddie's right. Eddie knew him from auditions as Leonard O'Hara. "It's the biggest part any sophomore got."

Easy for that goon to say, thought Eddie. Leonard had landed the role of Captain von Trapp.

"Rolf perfect for you," Duck contended. "He match your boyish face. He even sing song."

"Since when did you become a casting director?" Eddie responded.

Eddie had been told all his life he had golly gee-whiz features. Strangers normally guessed him to be two to three years younger than he was. Some compared him to that kid on *Silver Spoons. What was his name? . . .* Ricky Schroeder. They'd comfort him by saying he'd be grateful for his looks when he was fifty. Folks would think he was thirty. It was little comfort for a teenager.

During first period, while his history teacher lectured on Athens and Sparta, Eddie skimmed the script to locate every mention of Rolf Gruber. The guy had nineteen lines—two of which were a single word, like *Heil!* Three scenes, one song— a duet—and . . . hold on a second.

What was this? A kissing scene!

Wellll now! This changes everything!

The character whose mouth he was destined to suckle was Leisl, the oldest daughter of Captain von Trapp.

Eddie was convinced this experience would be much different from the one he'd had with that little actress in the seventh grade. *Now I've had practice!*

Maybe we'll hit it off, this girl and I, Eddie imagined. *Maybe we'll have one of those infamous "backstage" romances! No, that's impossible. I love Tanya. I must be true to my love! And yet . . . I wonder if she's pretty . . .*

When the bell rang, Eddie bounded down the hall like an antelope. Seconds later, his finger was again sliding down the cast of characters. Upon finding the name Leisl he followed it over to discover the name of his partner in passion.

Leisl . . . . Monica LaRoche.

Eddie's face went flush. His shoulders drooped to the level of his belly button. The letters of the name seemed to swell on the poster, growing, growing, growing, like a horrible, hungry monster. *No . . . this can't be right!* One more time, he found Leisl on the character list and followed the line over. The monster still drooled.

This is a joke! Some tasteless, cruel, evil, obnoxious, childish joke! Eddie felt dizzy. He had to sit down. Where was a chair when he needed one?

He'd seen her at tryouts that first night. She sang, "My Favorite Things," vying for the part of Maria, like every other girl. But Monica LaRoche hadn't been on the callback list. He thought he was *sure* of it.

And just when Eddie Fanta had started to think the world was revolving his way. Today was the first day in over a month he hadn't come to school in Louis Kosserinski's burdensome jacket. For the first time, he traded in his sweatshirt for a stylish button-up. Everyone standing around his locker that morning did a double take.

Mikey Swearingen didn't even show up to school the day after his confrontation with Eddie. Rumors were rampant that Eddie Fanta had messed him up good. Some of the stories were wildly conflicting, but there was one detail which everyone felt certain was true. Mikey's reported dark purple shiner was Eddie's handiwork for sure. During P.E., every acquaintance Eddie had made since entering this school swarmed around him as if they were lifelong buddies, begging for details.

Eddie responded to them with: "Suffice it to say, I don't expect any more trouble from a certain species of venomous reptile."

At least for today, Eddie was right. All Copperheads kept their distance. But the words they whispered were anything but docile. There was no way Eddie could have fully known the chain of events he set in motion the night he humiliated Mikey Swearingen. Never had the Copperhead leader harbored such a vicious hatred toward another human being. His zeal for vengeance was destined to choke every other ambition. Emotions had only to brew a little longer. Just a little longer . . .

* * * *

During that first evening of rehearsal, Eddie avoided even glancing at Monica. Practice was held in the auditorium. Most of the first rehearsal was an orientation on the director's "vision." Since the play opened the second week in December, it would have a distinct Christmasy feel.

Monica sat on the far end of the front row with two other Von Trapp daughters. Out of the corner of his eye, Eddie was certain he'd seen her peek back at him. He could just guess what she was thinking. It undoubtedly was jubilation over fulfilling her lifelong dream of smooching Eddie Fanta. Eddie shuddered when he thought about it.

When the meeting was over, Dave Walker, the junior who'd stolen Eddie's part of Max Detweiler, nudged his side and indicated Monica. She was busily gathering up her books and sweater.

"You lucky dog," he whispered. "She's *hot!*"

"Hot? Monica? Are you kidding me?"

Dave gave him the "OK" sign while winking. Eddie looked at Monica again. He looked her up and down in a way he never had before. *Monica LaRoche? Hot?* Such was also the assessment Duck had presented. What was it they saw that he didn't?

She was wearing a silky black skirt that hugged tight at her knees. Her long legs ended in lavender pumps. The day had grown much warmer so she tied her purple-black sweater over the top of her blouse. Then she gathered her shoulder bag into her arms.

Eddie tried, but in his mind's eye it was just too difficult to see beyond the frumpy, pug-nosed little girl who'd haunted him all those years in grade school. Clearly, she was no longer frumpy. Her nose was still small, but for some reason, it *worked* now. Eddie strained hard to remember exactly what it was about her that had repulsed him so. She even *moved* differently, like . . . well, like a girl.

When she turned around, Eddie was embarrassed to have

been caught gaping so intently. Monica smiled and stepped over.

"Eddie! Good to see you again. Looks like you and I have a lot of work ahead of us."

"Yeah," Eddie replied. His mouth groped for something to add, but failed.

Monica glanced at her watch. "Well, gotta go. See you Monday."

"Yeah," Eddie repeated, turning to watch as she exited the auditorium. "See you Monday."

Eddie desperately needed a third, fourth, and maybe even a fifth opinion on this matter. His newfound popularity as the boy who'd punched out Mikey Swearingen earned him a ride home with a couple other cast members. While en route, he asked them what they thought of Monica LaRoche. Jasper Wittingham, who played Franz the butler, made the same reference to her temperature as Dave Walker, calling her "hot." Jim Detrich, who was Admiral von Schreiber, placed her in the animal kingdom as a "fox," while Arlan Kimball, who played Friedrich, hurled her all the way back to infancy as a "babe." The consensus was blindingly clear. Any of them would trade places with Eddie Fanta in the blink of an eye.

There were only eight weeks of rehearsal before opening night. On Monday, the cast read dialogue, but by Tuesday, the company had been broken down into shifts. Those whose scenes weren't being blocked worked with Mr. Hagar, the musical director, or ran lines with Anne, Mr. Kasznar's assistant. It was a grueling project and unfortunately, Eddie's friendship with Duck suffered a bit. Eddie always seemed to be at school rehearsing or helping with the sets.

About the only thing Eddie didn't slack up on was Louis. Every night he'd read him another couple chapters of the *Book of Mormon* and accept a short list of errands. Louis's mood always brightened in Eddie's presence. The things he said were always a bit bizarre and obscure, but Eddie had been around enough old folks at the nursing home to know he should take it all with a grain of salt.

"How goes the mission?" he would ask.

"What mission is that, Mr. Kosserinski?"

"All men have a mission, though few so prestigious as yours. How is the jacket? Has it abolished fear? Has it changed the world?"

"It's changed *my* world," Eddie replied.

Louis smiled. "Press on."

Eddie wondered if there was something else Louis expected of him. He asked about the jacket so often, Eddie started to fear the old man might want it back. The time the boy spent wearing it had dropped drastically. Only once or twice a week did he even take it to school anymore, usually to make his geometry class considerably shorter (geometry was the one class where he could be sure no one would call on him) or to give him ample time to get back to school if he'd taken an extra long lunch.

The last week in October, the hallways were burgeoning with decorations for Jordan View's Homecoming. Homecoming was the only formal dance sophomores could attend without an upper-class escort. Festivities were one week away, leaving Eddie with the immediate prospect of finding a date or throwing in the towel. He was understandably gun-shy about approaching anyone, considering his last attempt at wooing a female. Nevertheless, he made a list one afternoon in Biology.

There was Liz Fairchild, whom he sat behind in English, but he'd seen her once with a boyfriend. There was Mitzi Buckingham, but she'd repeatedly voiced an addiction to football players. Then there was Tanya. *Oh*, that he could have asked Tanya, but she was acting more attached to Mikey Swearingen than ever.

The name that kept repeating in his head was Monica LaRoche, but Eddie still wasn't sure what to make of her. The conflict between past and present still clouded things somewhat. He was beginning to think he should ask her *only* because he could be reasonably sure she'd say yes. Heck, why not make a little girl's dream come true?

Eddie and Monica had yet to do the ole' "lip-lock" during

rehearsal. Every time they reached the last stanza of the "You Are Sixteen" number, when the kiss was to be executed, Eddie faked it by leaning forward and smooching the air.

Monica tried not to take it personally, but by the end of the second week, it was hard to ignore. Mr. Kasznar pulled Eddie aside and made it quite clear that if he didn't kiss her the next time they rehearsed his scene, he was going to assemble the whole cast to watch as he ordered *her* to kiss *him*, which Eddie decided might inflict serious damage to his manhood.

The same night they were to kiss was also the night they all were to have their dialogue memorized. All blocking was to be done without scripts. Eddie was so nervous about the kiss, he flubbed each line. Anne, cuing him at the edge of the proscenium, grew quite impatient.

"Well, your father's pretty Austrian," Anne quoted for him.

"Well," Eddie repeated, trying to add dramatic emphasis as he gazed into Monica's eyes, "your father *is* pretty Austrian."

"We're all Austrian," said Monica, delivering her line perfectly.

Eddie continued to gape at Monica, his mouth stuck at half-mast.

"Some people think we ought to be German," cued Ann.

"Some people think we sho—*ought to*—be German," said Eddie. He tried to continue, "They're pretty mad at those who think ... those who think ..."

"—pretty mad at those who don't think so!" raged Ann.

"Enough!" announced the director. "Let's go on to Scene Nine. *You two!* Go home and run lines together. We'll do your scene first thing tomorrow. Go! Go!"

Monica jumped up from the bench and marched off the stage. Eddie followed after her.

"I'm sorry," he mumbled.

Monica continued up the theatre aisle. "You knew your lines better two weeks ago."

"I said I was sorry," defended Eddie.

Monica snatched up her bag and sweater from the seat. "So where are we going to run lines? Your house or my house?"

Eddie stammered, "Uh, well—"

Monica interrupted, "My brothers and sisters won't give us a moment's peace at my house. What about yours?"

"I guess we could go there. My mom's been working until nine lately."

Monica continued conversing in an all-business tone, "Great! Do you have a car?"

"I don't."

"Then we'll take mine." She led the way to the parking lot.

"I didn't know you drove," Eddie commented, trying to keep up to her. "Are you sixteen?"

"Yep. Just like the song says."

"How come you're not a Junior?"

"I repeated the fourth grade."

Open mouth, insert foot, Eddie thought. They said nothing further until Monica found her '84 Accord and unlocked it. As Eddie seated himself beside Monica, he felt miserably self-conscious. Monica sensed it. It made her temper boil.

"Look!" she snapped, before starting the engine. "I don't like this any more than you do. I know how you feel about me. I've known *exactly* how you've felt about me since the fifth grade. But there's no way I'm gonna stand on that stage opening night and be made a fool of by some bonehead who can't remember a half dozen lines!"

Eddie had never been on a sinking ship, but he was confident he knew what it felt like. He tried to recall earth's lowest form of life. *A slug—no, an amoeba.* Whatever it was, Eddie could relate to such creatures in a way he never had before. *Maybe my Homecoming plans were a bit hasty.*

The icy silence between them ended when Eddie said, "Nineteen."

"Excuse me?"

"Nineteen. I have more than a half dozen lines. I have nineteen."

Monica laughed, but it wasn't because she thought Eddie was funny.

Eddie sighed deeply. Every skin cell on his body was itching, almost ringing. He hadn't felt this unusual sensation since the day his father left home.

He turned to Monica, "You don't have to run lines with me. I'll do it by myself and I *promise*, I'll have everything perfect by tomorrow." Eddie stepped out of Monica's car, but before he closed the door, he added, "A few weeks ago I wondered if it might be possible to travel back in time and change some of the mistakes I've made. I want you to know, one of the many things I'd try to make right is the way I used to treat you. I'm sorry, Monica. Good night."

Eddie left Monica in the darkened car. As far as he knew, she didn't start the ignition and pull away the whole time he walked toward the bus stop.

* * * *

The next afternoon, Eddie did much better with his dialogue, but he wasn't perfect. He still had to be cued on a couple lines and he flubbed up the second verse of "You Are Sixteen." But at the end of the song, after Monica kicked off Leisl's concluding dance step, Eddie grabbed her around the waist in a fashion which left her spellbound and kissed her as passionately as Rhett ever kissed Scarlet. Then he released her, exiting stage with his old-fashioned prop bicycle.

The cast and crew erupted with applause. Mr. Kasznar was shouting "Bravo! Bravo! Do that opening night and you'll bring down the house!"

After rehearsal, Eddie took too long getting ready to go and missed his usual ride. As he made the dark journey to his faithful old bus stop, Monica's car pulled into the gutter beside him. Her passenger window was open.

"Hey buddy!" she called to him, imitating a New York cabby, "which way 'eh ya goin'?"

Eddie stepped over and looked in the window. "Can you take me to Jersey?"

"Sure I can. But I gotta warn ya. I charge double what the meter says when I go outta town."

"Then how 'bout 23rd South and Redwood."

"*Now* you're tawkin'. Hop in."

As they pulled back into the street, Monica reminded him of his memory lapses during rehearsal. "Perfect, huh?"

"I swear I had it perfect this morning," Eddie claimed.

"Well, after tonight," Monica promised, "you're gonna say your lines forwards, backwards, sideways, and diagonally."

"Sounds like a plan."

While Eddie made them both a sandwich, Monica wandered through the Fanta's apartment, studying photographs and picking up knick-knacks. Eddie's bedroom door was open. She turned on the light and found herself mesmerized by the paintings and spaceships.

Eddie found her in his bedroom doorway.

She pointed. "Did you paint those yourself?"

Eddie nodded.

"You're really good."

"Thanks."

She noted the ceiling, "Captain Picard and Jacques Cousteau, huh?"

"Thems my heroes," said Eddie.

"Really? My ceiling is wallpapered with Tom Talon, the movie star. Your heroes, huh? Interesting. Both Frenchmen. Are you partial to French people, Eddie Fanta?"

"I never thought about it."

Eddie was a little slow tonight. He didn't catch the connection between French people and Monica *LaRoche* until five minutes later.

After their snack, they sat on the living room couch, drilling each of Eddie's lines twenty times. After a while, Eddie started getting worse instead of better.

"You have a lot more lines than I do," Eddie observed. "How do *you* keep it all straight?"

"My dad says I have a semiphotographic memory," she replied. "I never forget a name or a face. It's weird sometimes. I remember when I was younger and *really* into television, I could watch reruns during the summer and recite every line right along with the characters."

"That's amazing!"

"Not really. Your art talents—now *that's* amazing. Your painting of Saturn looks almost like a Voyager snapshot."

"Tell me something," Eddie chanced. "If you have such a good memory, how come you got sent back in the fourth grade?"

"I didn't get sent back. I *asked* to be sent back."

"Whatever for?"

"Oh, I told my parents a lot of tall tales. How the girls were picking on me. How I couldn't concentrate. I *did* manage straight F's my last two months, but that was deliberate."

"You gave up a whole year of your life? Why?"

Monica smiled and hid her face behind a couch pillow. "You don't want to know." She laughed nervously.

Eddie laughed with her, "Sure I do."

Monica set down the pillow. Her face went almost somber, then she said, "Because *you* were in the fourth grade and that was the year I met you."

Eddie's expression froze. Monica couldn't read him and it intimidated her terribly. She tried to brush it all off with, "Kids can do some pretty stupid things sometimes, huh?"

Eddie's expression hadn't changed. All his memories of a nutty, obsessive little girl came flooding back. He could see how vulnerable it had made her to tell this secret. Torn between his awkwardness and not wanting to hurt her feelings, he leaned forward and tried to deliver a kiss. She avoided it knowing it had been inspired by the wrong emotions.

"I have to go," she announced.

Eddie knew he'd done something wrong; he just wasn't quite sure what it was. As Monica stood, he stood with her.

"Wait, Monica," he pleaded. In hopes of smoothing over his blunder, he looked in her eyes and requested, "Will you go with me to Homecoming?"

"I can't," she replied. "I've already been asked."

Now Eddie's face was flush—but more with anger than embarrassment. "*You've what!*"

"Sorry," she said casually.

"By who?" Eddie demanded.

Monica was clearly ruffled by this interrogation, "Leonard O'Hara—if you must know. Captain von Trapp."

Ten seconds later, she was out the door, leaving Eddie to wonder for the rest of the night what had just happened.

*   *   *   *

It seemed fate had decreed before the foundations of the world that Eddie Fanta would fail in his efforts to find a date for Homecoming his sophomore year. Eddie's experience with Monica convinced him women were like a puzzle which comes with promising, informative directions but in the end proves absolutely unsolvable.

"How," he asked himself a number of times, "can a girl who admits she loved me enough to repeat a year of her life and who hints up and down that her feelings haven't changed, reject me so brutally?"

Eddie's depression was clinched when Duck confessed *he'd* approached a girl about Homecoming—and she'd accepted!

"You mean you're going to the dance?" Eddie asked. *"Without me?"*

"I rent tux and everything," Duck admitted. "Her name Yen Phok. She Vietnamese and *boy* do she have legs."

Eddie thought back on the bet he and Duck had made the previous summer. Though Eddie was the first to successfully kiss a girl, Duck was the first to land a date. Eddie may have won a battle, but Duck was definitely winning the war.

His only comfort that night, as he sat home devouring a full bag of *Doritos*, was the radio's report that Jordan View had lost the game twenty-eight to zip. Now, maybe the whole school would join in his misery.

Later, he went over to Louis's house for the old man's nightly dose of scriptures. They'd made it to Alma, Chapter 11, which discusses the resurrection and the reuniting of body and spirit. Eddie read verse forty-four: *"Now, this restoration shall come to all, both old and young, both bond and free, both male and female, both the wicked and the righteous; and even there shall not so much as a hair of their heads be lost . . ."*

Eddie glanced up at Louis, who was still wearing the hooded sweatshirt to hide the greater part of his burns and disfigurement. The old man was looking off into space.

"I'll bet that's your favorite verse, eh?" Eddie commented. When Louis didn't reply right away, Eddie grew embarrassed for having made such a touchy observation.

"No," Louis retorted. "My favorite verse is Ether 12, verse 27." He quoted verbatim. *"And if men come unto me, I will show unto them their weakness. I give unto men weakness that they may be humble, and my grace is sufficient for all men who humble themselves before me; for if they humble themselves before me, and have faith in me, then I will make weak things become strong unto them."*

His voice trailed off toward the end. When he was finished, he closed his eyes.

Eddie didn't get it. The verse made it sound like the Lord *enjoyed* seeing people make fools of themselves. As if the reason Eddie's parents were screwups and the reason Tanya hated him and the reason Louis looked like a wraith from a nightmare was a ploy to make everyone bow down and be humble. Was this supposed to explain all the sadness in the world? The Lord just trying to make people humble? Well, Eddie had news for the Lord: *It isn't working!*

It just makes people bitter and hateful and depressed. If this is God's way, Eddie decided, God is cruel . . . cataclysmically *cruel.*

But Eddie wouldn't dishonor Louis by stating his opinion out loud.

He said, "My weakness is understanding girls. I have no idea how the Lord is supposed to make *that* one strong. What *I* need to know is what they're thinking before *and* after they open their mouths. 'Cause it's never the same."

Louis turned and faced him. "Did I hear you say you seek knowledge, Edward Fanta?"

"Sure, I guess," Eddie replied. "Especially if it gets girls."

Louis's eyes sparkled like Christmas lights. "I can help

you, Edward. But first I must tell you, you're absolutely wrong. God is *not* cataclysmically cruel. Weakness plus humility plus faith equals strength. This has always been God's formula."

Eddie didn't hear a single word Louis uttered beyond the phrase he'd promised himself would never escape the maximum security cells of his brain. *Did he just do what I think he did?*

"I didn't—I don't remember—did I say that out loud?"

"Not out loud," Louis replied, "but you said it just the same."

• *EIGHT* •

Eddie took a moment to absorb the resplendent harmony of glimmers and shadows, cogs and belts, until Louis had ridden down his self-designed wheelchair lift and managed to turn on the overhead lights. Again, the cellar made Eddie think of Frankenstein's laboratory—*only in this lab, Frankenstein and the so-called "monster" are one and the same.*

Eddie found himself swallowing hard. Had he forgotten so soon that moments ago Louis had read his mind? Embarrassed, he turned to the old man, who was wheeling toward him down the corridor.

"But this laboratory did not create *me*," responded Louis austerely to Eddie's thought. "I created *it*."

"Sorry," Eddie said meekly.

Ignoring him, Louis aimed his chair toward the cabinets along the wall. But before approaching them, he requested Eddie to look closely into his right ear. The boy did so and noticed a pea-sized object, shaped somewhat like a lop-sided bell.

"Is it a hearing aid?" Eddie wondered.

"It's a receiver. I was the first to make such a high-quality unit so compact. The very first."

"Is that how you listen to my thoughts?"

"I said it's only a receiver!" he scolded. "The translator/recorder is the primary mechanism. It homes in on synaptic impulses and translates them into an audible dialect."

"The *Uniglottal Neurological Translator!*" Eddie exclaimed. "I saw that name on one of these cabinets."

"That's the portable unit. The one I use is hooked into the mainframe. Mine has a larger range—three-quarters of a mile. The portable unit is useless beyond seventy-five yards. When I recorded the electro-wave discharges of your brain the night you were attacked in front of my gate, all I had to do was feed the information into the *Translator.*"

Eddie was stunned. "You mean you've been listening to my thoughts for two months?" He felt strangely violated.

"I've listened only when you were under my roof. After all, this is my property. Be grateful. I could have read them anytime you were within three-quarters of a mile."

Hesitantly, Eddie asked, "What do I think about? I mean, do I think some pretty stupid thoughts?"

"Yes," Louis answered matter-of-factly. "Too many to count. Undisciplined frivolity!" He grew pensive. "There are moments though. Promising moments."

Eddie wondered, "If you can receive thoughts from three-quarters of a mile, how far can you send them? Like when you 'call' someone?"

"As far and as fast as light can travel."

"Even to another planet?"

"Of course not! The signal would become too weak to read much beyond the Earth's atmosphere. These machines merely enhance a natural, though usually suffocated, capability inherent in everyone's psyche. This is how a mother knows a child half way around the globe has experienced a terrible accident. This is how God receives prayer. It's how he transmits revelation. All God's miracles are strictly extensions of natural law. One day we will understand and duplicate every one of them."

As Louis spoke, Eddie wandered before each of the cabinets. The only other one with a full title read *Neurological Manipulator: Enmity/Affinity.* But Eddie ignored that cabinet for the time being, as well as the others. He focused on the cabinet on the end—the dusty steel case fortified with six rusting padlocks.

"What's in this one?" Eddie asked. He drew the first letter of his name in the dust on top.

When he turned around, Louis's expression was difficult to interpret. Was he actually . . . trembling?

"It's nothing," Louis answered. "Don't ask about it."

Eddie's shoulders drooped. Louis knew Eddie's thoughts. *Overcurious little whelp.* Louis felt obliged to explain. "I'll tell you once, but never again. Discussing it is a waste of my time. It's called a *Universal Forces Agglomerative Harmonizer.* I built it a short time back to test a theory of mine. It's a law in quantum physics that imperfection cannot coexist with perfection or order with disorder. Since God's kingdom is reputedly perfect, the reason a corrupt soul cannot dwell there might have as much to do with physics as final judgments. When man seeks perfection, he is in essence seeking to harmonize himself with all of the fundamental forces of nature—electromagnetism, the strong and weak forces of atomics, gravity. . . . My theory stated that the pursuit of perfection could be enhanced by preharmonizing these universal forces with an individual's brain wave emissions. Many Eastern philosophies purport similar possibilities. In other words, I wondered if I could form a conduit around an individual which directly influences changes for that individual's benefit."

Eddie strained to comprehend. Louis was speaking as if to a colleague instead of a boy who'd be lucky to get a "C" in physical science.

"Let me get this straight," Eddie said. "You say you were trying to improve your chances for getting into heaven?"

"No, no!" Louis impatiently clarified. "The recipe for that achievement is faith! Repentance! Obedience! But even the most stalwart Christian—or every other religionist for that matter—avoids, or never has the chance to face, the situations which provide them with the greatest leaps of spiritual attainment. It's human nature to pray only for happiness—to seek only comfort. Yet, these very luxuries can *hinder* us, Edward. The *Harmonizer* was meant to tailor fate—force us to face every growth promoting situation which our individual personalities might require. My theory was sound, but its practical application was . . . unsound."

"So you're saying if a person's greatest personal attainment would come from being elected president, this thing was supposed to help bring it to pass?"

"Or if such growth would only come through becoming a decrepit, gutter-scraping bum, the *Harmonizer* was meant to help bring *this* to pass as well. But, alas, there were certain problems I could never quite conquer."

"If it doesn't work, how come it's locked up?"

"Are you insane! The unit is desperately unstable! That cabinet's casing is six solid inches of lead. If it weren't, the exposure would boil us both like rats in a microwave—from the inside out."

Eddie removed his hand from the cabinet as from a hot stove. He made sure no radiation burns or deformities had shown up on his palm. The cabinet was only two feet square. Losing six inches from every side meant this object was very small indeed.

Louis returned to the subject at hand by wheeling over to the cabinet marked *Uniglottal Neurological Translator* and opening its door. This particular invention was in two attachable parts. The largest section was designed to home in and record brain frequencies. The other part was a square box, shaped much like a radio. It even had dials for volume. This was the actual *Translator*. After a particular frequency had been fed into it from the recorder, it could be detached and hung on the belt like a *Walkman*. To hear the relayed message, Eddie could either use earphones or the other pea-sized, ear-canal receiver which Louis dropped in his hand. It was Eddie's second Christmas already this year—and snow hadn't even fallen!

The *Translator* and its recorder were quite a bit more complicated than the jacket and Louis spent the next hour explaining how to use it, scolding whenever the boy didn't grasp his instructions at once. Eddie adjusted the triangulating antennas and aimed the mechanism at Louis from across the room. The old man's brain pattern took the form of colorful flashes and designs on the unit's miniature monitor window. A tiny red light ignited to confirm that the pattern was recorded. Eddie then fed the information into the *Translator*.

Louis taught Eddie how to reboot a pattern once it was captured by assigning it a four-letter code, usually the first initial of the person's first name and the beginning three letters of their last name. At present, the only human patterns logged into the memory were that of Louis, Eddie, and Ray Fayle. When Louis said "go," the thought he sent Eddie across the *Translator* was: *Now the mission has expanded, Edward Fanta. Now you must also abolish ignorance in the world. Nothing will be unknowable. Nothing will be secret.*

Eddie cringed inwardly. Whenever Louis got into his "mission" mode, the boy became terribly nervous. But could the old man be right? Was something this small really capable of such miracles?

After Louis had sent his brief selection of thoughts, Eddie's earpiece went silent. The boy realized the unit couldn't read *all* brain functions; only those with the strongest output—the words people say in their head. When thoughts were free-flowing—without subverbalization—the message over the *Translator* became jumbled, only snatches of words or phrases. In Louis's case, the message had dissolved into total static, proving that people could choose not to have their mind read at all.

If such an invention were ever sold on the market, people would have to learn to adjust to a completely new pattern of cogitation. The court systems would change; judges and juries would start giving as much credence to what witnesses were *thinking*, as to what they were *saying*. Parents would buy *Neurological Translators* out of necessity the moment their kids became teenagers. Teachers would start telling mischievous children to keep their thoughts to themselves. Jealous girlfriends would inform boyfriends that in spite of what the boyfriend might be saying, she could hear what he was thinking "loud and clear!" A whole new vocabulary would have to be adopted.

Victims of a crime might more easily verify a perpetrator's tendencies and take advance action. Criminals would have to learn to bury their thoughts deep in their hearts, never subverbalizing a single word of their wicked intentions.

But for now, Eddie Fanta held in his arms the only portable unit in existence. With the receiver in his ear, a *Walkman*-looking thing on his belt, and the recorder apparatus in his school knapsack, who would suspect? As Eddie left Louis's house, he was already planning to have a heyday.

*   *   *   *

"So how was the dance?" Eddie asked Duck when he arrived home at a quarter past midnight. Eddie had recorded Duck's brain pattern as he strolled up the front walk. His friend was still clad in his tuxedo.

"It very nice," Duck replied. *Much better than I expected,* Eddie heard over the receiver.

"Did you kiss her?"

"A gentleman never tell." *Three times.*

"You kissed her three times?"

Duck's eyes widened, "How you know that?" *Was he spying on me the whole night?*

"No, I wasn't spying."

Did she call and tell you?

"No, she didn't call either."

Oh, my heavens! He knows what I'm thinking!

"Exactly!" Eddie confirmed.

Eddie unveiled the *Translator.* Duck wasn't quite as flabbergasted with this contraption as he was with the jacket. Nothing Eddie Fanta came up with surprised him anymore. But Eddie did catch him thinking: *My first kiss and this all in one night.*

The excitement left them both insomniacs. Duck changed clothes and the two of them walked up the street to watch all the late-night comers and goers at 7-11 while sitting on a curb in the empty bank parking lot across the street. Eddie would home-in on a particular individual and then listen on his tiny ear receiver while Duck listened through the earphones.

A guy who walked inside to pay for his gas couldn't seem to get the lyrics of the song on his car radio out of his head. Another man who stood next to the pay phone kept repeating in his mind: *Why should I call? If she wants me back, she knows how to find me. I'm not gonna play her games any longer.*

The girl working behind the counter was quite heavyset, but that didn't hinder her imagination from guessing what a date might be like with every guy who entered the store: *He'd be nice. Probably married. Yup, there's the ring. He's too old. Now, that one's a hunk. I need to get another roll of quarters soon. How come he didn't say anything? Rude, rude, rude.*

Eddie felt sorry for her. He switched to a cowboy hopping out of his pickup: *Okay, it's over. Man! that was close. Coulda had a heart attack. Maybe it's time I choose one or the other. Maybe. But I can't choose. Just gotta be more careful . . .*

They listened to a lady who sat alone in the car while her husband went in for cigarettes: *Just be calm. Calm. He won't hurt me if I'm calm. Maybe he'll pass out if I drive slow. Everything will be fine. Just hang in there, girl. You can take a couple more slaps . . .*

Duck took off the earphones, "This not right, Eddie."

"What's the matter?"

"Thoughts are private. We eavesdropping!"

Eddie thought about it. Then he justified, "It's not like we're ever gonna see these people again. Who knows? We might even hear something that could save somebody's life."

"It depressing! Everybody so sad and angry!"

"It's just an off night."

Despite Duck's flash of conscience, he couldn't quash the temptation. Again he donned the earphones. Eddie and Duck sat across the street until 3:00 A.M., listening to everyone's thoughts from a twelve-year-old boy as he contemplated stealing a candy bar, then changed his mind, to a lonely old man who walked up to the 7-11 just to find somebody to talk to. When the cashier brushed him off, he wandered home again, thinking of a wife eleven years gone and times gone by when people weren't so busy.

Dragging their feet back to the duplex, both Duck *and* Eddie felt nauseated by guilt. Eddie wanted to hit the code which allowed him to hear Duck's thoughts exactly but he didn't have the nerve, and besides, he pretty much knew what the Cambodian was thinking anyway.

When Louis gave him the *Translator*, did he expect it to be used so indiscreetly, eavesdropping on the world? He should have realized, Eddie was fifteen—the age when every question *must* be answered, every mystery solved—despite the consequences. Louis may not have remembered what it was like to be fifteen. That is, if someone of his genius ever really was.

Eddie got through the entire weekend without succumbing to the urge to read anyone else's mind. But by Sunday night, his imagination was again reeling with the possibilities.

Responsibility, Eddie decided. *That's the factor I never internalized. Like when I listened to the thoughts of that lonesome old man. If I'd made an effort to talk to him, been kind to him for a while, hearing his thoughts would have been a good thing, wouldn't it?*

So Eddie justified bringing the *Translator* to school Monday by committing to offer relief every time he heard painful thoughts. What could be nobler? He'd be a kind of comic book superhero, or like that Michael Landon angel dude on *Highway to Heaven.*

As it turned out, Eddie exerted most of his energy toward recording the brain waves of every pretty girl in sight. He couldn't believe some of the things girls thought about. Conspiracy against other girls was common. Put downs for petty things like fashion and makeup were epidemic. They even thought about sex from time to time, though Eddie found that boys generally dominated the corner on that market. The most disappointing thing Eddie found was that very few girls spent a whole lot of time thinking about *him.*

He'd felt sure Brenda Toone in history daydreamed about him, but instead, all her thoughts were consumed by the geek sitting one desk up. Eddie successfully wheedled a thought from Mitzi Buckingham which confirmed that she thought he was cute, but her follow up thought was: *Too bad I could never date him. It wouldn't look good, dating a sophomore.*

Whenever anyone asked about the gizmo he kept pointing at everyone, Eddie dispelled their curiosity by calling it a science project, measuring humidity, or light, or whatever. Duck found Eddie at lunch and gave him a judgmental eye, but when Eddie told him he'd captured the thoughts of Yen Phok, his Homecoming date, the Cambodian's ears promptly perked.

Eddie revealed, "She thinks you're a—and I quote—'tasty hunk.'"

Duck suddenly forgot the ethics speech he'd planned to deliver to his friend.

During rehearsal, Eddie recorded the brain waves of every cast member. It was amazing how many patterns the *Translator* could hold. He'd already coded over thirty and Louis had told him it would carry well over a hundred. Then it was only a matter of transferring the data into the mainframe in Louis's cellar.

What a pain trying to read the thoughts of Monica LaRoche! She didn't think verbally very often and when she did, it was only for a word or two. Then her mind flitted off somewhere else. Either she was uncommonly bright or a total airhead.

Eddie confronted her backstage one day while she waited for the entrance cue to one of her scenes without Rolf. It was the first time he'd approached her for a real conversation since the night she stormed out.

"How are ya?" he whispered.

She glanced at him. "I'm fine."

Eddie heard no further thought in his ear receiver, just the glint of a single phrase which included the word "cautious."

"So did you have fun last weekend?"

"Yes, I did." Monica faced forward again, listening for her cue.

Eddie pressed further. "Did you enjoy the dance?"

"Uh huh."

Boy, this girl was exasperating! Eddie didn't hear a single thought which confirmed or denied or expounded her statements.

"Has he asked you out again?"

"Yes. But what business is that of yours?"

"No business at all, but . . . well, I feel it's my responsibility to tell you, as a friend: Leonard O'Hara isn't the right guy for you."

Monica turned back slowly and deliberately, "Oh really? And what makes you think I need *your* help deciding which guys are right or wrong for me?"

At last! Eddie heard one of her thoughts: *You've got some nerve, Eddie Fanta.* "Monica, listen. Everything in Leonard's head is X-rated. He'd never do right by you. Just a moment ago he was contemplating taking out Stephanie Ogden."

"And how is it you've come to know all this? Are you a mind reader now, Eddie Fanta?"

"As a matter—" Eddie stopped himself. "Let me just say, I know for a fact he only views you as this month's 'sophomore conquest.'"

Monica's jaw dropped. The statement sounded a little too much like Leonard's true style of wording. The thought which echoed in Eddie's ear receiver next was loud and clear: *How dare that vermin go around talking about me like that!*

When Monica looked back onto the stage, she noticed that the entire Von Trapp family was awaiting her entrance. The director called out, "Leisl, where are you?"

As Eddie watched her march out from the wing, he could almost see her trail of steam. Leonard O'Hara continued with his next line, oblivious to the oncoming locomotive.

"This is your new fraulein," Leonard said in the voice of his character, Captain von Trapp. "Fraulein Maria. As I sound your signal—"

But Leonard never got the prop whistle into his mouth. Instead, he got a taste of Monica's knuckle. She didn't slap him as anyone might have expected. She punched him! And Leonard O'Hara actually staggered.

The evening's rehearsal of this particular scene was duly postponed.

*   *   *   *

The last couple mornings, Eddie had noted a new smell in the bathroom. Perfume—an expensive kind. The bottle in the medicine cabinet read *Georgio*. His mother hadn't worn perfume for months. Least of all a kind normally reserved for places slightly more formal than the office.

On Saturday evening, after spending a good hour primping in front of the mirror, she announced plans to attend a business dinner, but Eddie had homed in on her with the *Translator*. Her thoughts reported something completely different: *I have a date. I don't know why I think I have to lie to my son. Enough time has passed. He'd understand.*

A car pulled into the driveway and honked.

How tactless, Eddie thought. *He won't even come to the door.* Then he realized this was probably at his mother's request.

Eddie didn't utter a word as he watched her leave the apartment. For the next hour, he stared mindlessly at ESPN. *How should I feel about this?* Eddie wondered. If only he could aim the *Translator* at himself and understand his *own* thoughts.

When Eddie went over to Louis's that evening, the old man perceived his thoughts immediately. "Why do you trouble your mind with such superfluous things?" he rebuked.

Eddie started to glower at Louis, then turned away. Though it may have felt okay to read the thoughts of others, it wasn't always so comfortable to have someone reading his own.

"My family is not superfluous. You don't understand. My mother is trying to be something she's not. It makes me sick! She's the most selfish, unforgiving person I know. My dad was completely willing to change his ways to meet her standards and she . . . she spat in his face!"

"All tragedies have two sides," Louis stated. "You mustn't let bitterness obscure your focus on the mission."

"Well, I've never heard my mother's side," said Eddie. "She's never told it. Which is just as well. I can't trust my mother. She even lied about where she was going tonight!"

"You may not see as much as you think," Louis observed.

"Oh, is that so?" Eddie snapped. "Have you captured my mother's brain pattern, too? And my father's? Have you listened in on the whole lousy universe? What do you know about people? You've only met two in the last forty years!"

Louis drew back. "I know people," he choked out, his body shaking. "I know them. I know they can forget how to hear . . . I know they can forget how to see."

With his disfigured hands, Louis gripped the treads on his wheelchair. He rolled into a hallway at the other end of the room, leaving Eddie alone in the study. Eddie groaned. He joggled his head and blew the air out of his lungs. *I had no right to take out my frustrations on Louis like that.* Eddie climbed out of the recliner and followed Louis into the hallway. He wasn't in sight, but there was an open door at the end of the hall emitting light. Eddie approached the room, his steps making the floor creak.

The room was empty and barren. No carpeting, just old and scarred panels of wood. No windows. Not a stitch of furniture except for a tray at the far wall. Louis was beside this tray, mixing oil paint with an artist's brush, his hand trembling, his back to the doorway.

Stretched across the far wall was a mural—a life-size portrait of a postwar family of four. The three-by-five photograph on which it was based sat in a frame on the tray. Once upon a time, the photo had been torn in half. The scotch tape which held it together had yellowed.

Eddie's eyes were drawn to the painting—to the man in the center. A father of about thirty years. The young Louis Kosserinski wasn't at all how Eddie imagined. There was nothing brainy or awkward about this man. He was tall and commanding. The woman was equally striking, like pictures Eddie had seen of Grace Kelly. At one time the mural had apparently been finished, but an old water leak from the ceiling had made cracks in the plaster. There was a rust-colored stain running all the way to the floor. A new coat of plaster covered most of the damaged portions. Louis had already repainted his wife. Repairs on the youngest boy were all that remained.

Louis spoke without turning. "Swamp cooler leaked about two years ago. Ray fixed it for me."

Eddie stepped closer. The accuracy from photograph to painting was remarkable, except that the photo was black and white and the painting was color. Even so, Eddie's eye, trained by his own artistic abilities, noted a slight difference in quality between the old version and the repaired one, likely because of Louis's shaking hands and fading eyesight.

The old man was currently mixing dark red to touch up the cap on the littlest boy's head. "I'm not . . . I'm not quite sure if it was this dark or not. I've taken liberties."

Eddie noted that the two people damaged by the water were the same two which had left him forty years before.

"Where did they go? Your wife and the boy?" Eddie asked.

"East. She told me East. Her people were from the East."

"You never tried to find her?"

His hand still lightly trembling, Louis dabbed his color onto the wall. "She came into my hospital room. My jaw was wired shut so I couldn't reply. I'd taken her first son; and she was taking the other."

"You're probably better off that she left."

Louis paused. His eyes locked into those of his wife on the wall. "Whether in this life or the next, I look forward to the day I rejoin my family more than any other gift of Almighty God."

"Even your wife?"

"My wife was young. The doctors weren't sure I would live. Or if I lived, they didn't think I'd retain a sound mind for very long with such unending pain."

"I don't think that's any excuse at all."

"We were married in the Salt Lake Temple—sealed for time and all eternity."

"I wouldn't even think you and her were goin' to the same eternal place, if you know what I mean."

"Then I'll tire the ears of our Maker pleading her cause until the universe takes its last breath. Joseph Smith said he would do no less for his recalcitrant wife, Emma."

"Some things you shouldn't forgive," Eddie countered. "I may love my mother, but sometimes I wonder if I can *ever* forgive her."

"Your mother is not the one you need to forgive," Louis calmly retorted, "but you already know that."

The old man didn't look up, or even falter in his brush stroke. Eddie was bitterly tempted to demand what Louis meant, but the boy changed his mind and closed his mouth. Quietly, Eddie returned toward the door.

Looking back, Eddie said only, "I'll see you tomorrow."

Louis continued applying his paint. He didn't appear to have heard. Eddie turned away and left Louis's house.

Wandering home, Eddie felt a strange anger. Was it directed at Louis? His mother? He wasn't sure. With every passing step, the anger grew harsher. It climaxed when he arrived home and noticed that his mother was still out on the town.

What is it you want? Eddie asked himself. *Do you want her to wither into an old maid—would that make you happy? If she got married and gave you a new father, better than Dad ever was—would that make you happy?*

No, Eddie concluded.

I want my old family back. I want them back the way they were at Christmas when I was eight years old. Corny right? But that's what I really *want.*

Yet experience had taught Eddie that the things he truly wanted were most assuredly the things which could never be.

. . . Or could they?

Words flashed in Eddie's memory, almost revelatory, like a bolt of lightning through his bedroom window. The words belonged to one of the titles he'd seen etched on an invention cabinet in Louis's cellar. A cabinet without locks, but one whose contents he hadn't yet seen. *What was it again?* He strained to remember exactly how it went.

Neurological Manipulator: Enmity/Affinity.

Eddie wondered. He just wondered . . .

• *NINE* •

Eddie wouldn't risk asking Louis to hand over another invention. Louis was too unpredictable. It wasn't implausible to think such a request might shake him into demanding *all* the inventions back. Better to ask forgiveness than permission.

Eddie strapped on Louis's jacket. He stepped outside before accelerating to avoid ripping the front door off its hinges. It was after midnight now. Eddie's mother was still out with her mystery date. The October air had quite a bite, which only sharpened when Eddie turned the knobs inward.

Upon reaching Louis's iron gate, he contemplated twisting the knobs back so he wouldn't destroy anything. But the squeaky hinges would have alerted Louis like a fire siren. Retaining his accelerated perceptions, Eddie opened the gate, stepped inside, and pushed it closed behind him. He decelerated to normal time to assess the damage. *Thank goodness!* The iron and stone were remarkably sturdy. Nothing was bent or broken. At the cellar door he switched off the jacket, stepped inside, and switched it on again. He did the same when he reached the cabinet marked *Neurological Manipulator: Enmity/ Affinity.*

By normal clock time, Eddie obtained the *Manipulator* and returned home in less than one minute. He took it into his bedroom and studied it under his lamps, trying to decide if it looked more like a laser gun or a video camera. Perhaps neither, although the unit did have a trigger as well as a viewfinder. While peering through the viewfinder and simultaneously depressing the trigger, Eddie watched a series of indicators light up around the edge of the inner frame, just like his mother's 35mm camera. Most of the indicators were dormant. Eddie concluded from the symbols that the *Manipulator* would have to be aimed at something in order to be activated. Something with a brain. Probably a brain more advanced than an earthworm, although Louis's cat had clearly been a usable subject in the past.

What bothered Eddie was the fitting at the *Manipulator's* base suggesting it was designed to connect into something. There'd been nothing else with it in the cabinet.

Eddie gleaned that the fitting looked similar to the one on the recording unit of the *Translator*. He retrieved the brain wave recorder from his knapsack. Sure enough, the *Manipulator* snapped in elegantly. As an experiment, Eddie punched in the four-letter code for his own brain pattern. Then he hit the "feed" button, just as he would if the *Translator* had been attached instead of the *Manipulator*. Three seconds later, the "feed" button blinked out, indicating that the pattern transfer was complete. Eddie detached the *Manipulator*. Now to find a cerebral subject.

Across the fence lurked his neighbor's rottweiler, Adolf. This dog had hated Eddie from the day he moved in. When it watched him, a prime rib was mirrored in its eyes. The dog saw everyone that way, except maybe its owner—an all-night truck driver with a phobia for burglars.

Eddie went out the back door, ready to creep up to the fence. He needed to spot the dog within the *Manipulator's* viewfinder before it alerted the neighborhood. Unfortunately, its canine ears were perked the moment Eddie slid open the door. Barking commenced, which, of course, inspired every mutt within ten blocks to join in the chorus.

Eddie aimed the *Manipulator* through the thin space between the pickets while Adolf displayed his sharp fangs. A moment after he depressed the trigger, a red stripe at the bottom lit up.

To Eddie's astonishment, the dog's barking intensified. The animal appeared to regress into a demonic frenzy, smashing itself against the fence, its jaws gnawing at the wood.

Just like the cat, Eddie thought.

One of the pickets broke and the dog thrust its snout through the space. The nails on a second picket jolted loose. Eddie knew if he didn't do something fast, he'd lose his jugular.

He held the *Manipulator* away from his eye. There was a lever on the back of the unit which ran horizontally. The lever was positioned far to the left. He set it all the way to the right. Finding the dog in the viewfinder a second time, he depressed the trigger. Again, the red stripe below the viewframe illuminated.

The barking stopped. In its place, Eddie heard a doleful whimper. For the first time since Eddie had moved to this neighborhood, Adolf was wagging his tail and lapping up the venomous drool from his chin. Cautiously, Eddie approached the hole in the fence. He floated a quivering hand toward the animal's snout. Never had Eddie felt such gratitude from a dog—just to have the *honor* of licking his palm.

Eddie let out a hoot. *It works!*

The boy regretted not hearing Louis's explanation of the principles behind it. Had he been given such an opportunity, he would have heard how wave pulses of the brain pattern inside the *Manipulator* gun "stroked" synaptic connections inside the irritation or pleasure centers of the brain fired upon, releasing a powerful dose of neurological chemicals. The stimulation was not love or hate *per se*. All the recipient knew for sure was that when they were in the presence of the person whose brain pattern was inside the unit, or even when the recipient daydreamed about this person, they suddenly experienced intense feelings of pleasure or irritation. If the lever on the *Manipulator* gun was pulled all the way to the right or left, it might create an emotional response which exceeded every other level of love or hate the recipient had ever experienced.

Eddie heard a car pull into the driveway and idle its engine. He pulled his hand away from the licking canine and charged back into the house. Peering through a crack between the curtains, Eddie spied his mother and her date sitting in a *Nissan 300 ZX*, talking casually.

Eddie rushed back into his bedroom and grabbed the wave recording unit of the *Translator*. While his legs carried him back to the living room, his fingers reattached the *Manipulator*. Facing out the window, his knees in the couch cushion, Eddie lifted back the curtain. Without detaching the *Manipulator*, he aimed the recording unit at the stranger's silhouette. After a second, the recorder signified that it had captured the stranger's pattern.

"Gotcha!" Eddie whispered.

Quickly, Eddie fed the information into the *Manipulator* and threw the lever to the left—and not a moment too soon— because the beastly ogre was just leaning over to kiss his mother good night. Squinting into the viewfinder, Eddie placed his mother in the cross-hairs and pulled the trigger.

The severance of their lip-lock was more dramatic than Eddie had hoped. Mom used both arms to fend him off. She practically fell out of the car door backwards trying to escape. With the back of both her hands, she began wiping off her mouth and spitting, as if she'd kissed the slime on a salamander. The date got out of the car to watch her flee into the house. His palms turned upward, wondering what in blazes had caused her sudden revulsion. He began following her, but she slipped inside the door and locked it behind her. He knocked loudly.

"Go away!" she cried.

"Not until I get an explanation!" he called through the door.

"You *disgust* me! Get away from here!"

"You're *nuts* lady! Totally bonkers!"

After a moment the man screeched away in his sports car. Eddie's mother still had an expression of loathing and nausea when she turned to her son, now seated calmly on the couch.

"I can't believe I actually went out with that creep!" she exclaimed. "How could I do it?"

Eddie shrugged his shoulders, "Beats me, Mom."

He had a hard time suppressing a grin.

* * * *

Come Sunday, Eddie was rudely awakened from his afternoon nap by two dopey looking gentlemen in pressed shirts and ties who claimed to be home teachers. Eddie was sorely tempted to ask for I.D. They'd been living here for eight months and nobody with that title had ever dropped by before.

Mrs. Fanta invited Brother Schlyter and Brother Hurst to sit on the couch. Brother Schlyter wore coke-bottle glasses with a frame style out of the fifties and Brother Hurst was a typical product of the neighborhood—more hillbilly than city dweller.

"I just want to assure you," Brother Schlyter began, "we intend to be here every month without fail from now on."

"Sorry for not making it sooner," added Brother Hurst. "The ward's been making some adjustments and some of the new families hadn't gotten assigned."

Eddie rolled his eyes. *Adjusting for eight months, eh?*

"May I be excused a moment?" he asked his mother. Eddie pranced back to his bedroom and gathered up the recording unit and *Manipulator*. Upon returning, he told everyone all the high-tech gear was for a school project. "Don't mind me."

Heckle and Jeckle started teaching the lesson from the *Ensign*. Fearing that Brother Schlyter's promise of interrupting his Sunday naps every month might be sincere, Eddie began attaching the wave recorder.

He fed his own brain pattern into the *Manipulator*. About the time they began questioning him about school and hobbies, he zapped them. The lever was far to the left.

After paying Eddie a distasteful glance, they began directing their questions to Eddie's mother. Eddie fed his mother's brain pattern into the unit and zapped them both again. Afterwards, the home teachers started speedily wrapping things up.

To be ornery, Eddie captured Brother Schlyter's brain pattern and zapped Brother Hurst. Then he captured Brother Hurst's pattern and zapped Brother Schlyter.

It was hard to ignore the tension as the home teachers left. They had a lively spat as they walked toward their vehicle— so lively that Brother Hurst decided he'd rather walk home.

"Well, that was . . . interesting," commented Eddie's puzzled mother.

"See you next month!" Eddie called after them.

*   *   *   *

"So what's with all the technical junk?" asked one of Eddie's fellow students on Monday before history class began.

"It's a video camera and accessories," Eddie replied. "I'm practicing to take *Photography I*."

"Where's the video cassette supposed to go?"

Eddie sent him a scurvy look. "You don't expect me to use a *real* camera do you? I'm only practicing!"

Eddie was saved by the bell. Mr. Meister asked him to put his "toys" back into his knapsack, but not before Eddie had pulled the trigger with Brenda Toone in his sights. The lever, of course, was set to the right.

All through class, Brenda gawked at him in mesmerized awe. Every time Eddie looked back, she would simper long and deep as if a mere glance from Eddie had fulfilled her every dream.

No one was safe. Liz Fairchild broke up with her boyfriend during lunch. Mitzi Buckingham was cured of her addiction for football players. The principal became curiously infatuated with the school nurse and the widowed janitor appeared to have fallen for Miss O'Conner, the old-maid, Home-Ec teacher.

When final period let out, Eddie had fifteen of the school's most gorgeous women traipsing at his heels. They followed him to the stage doors.

"Sorry girls. I have rehearsal now," Eddie announced.

Moans of disappointment.

"But when will we see you again?" asked Brenda.

Leonard O'Hara walked by, giving Eddie strange looks. "Uh, I don't know," an embarrassed Eddie replied. "Tomorrow, I'm sure."

"The important thing is—" Mitzi Buckingham seductively wrapped her fingers around Eddie's biceps "—when will I see you *alone*."

The others scowled at Mitzi. If she'd tried anything else it may have broken out in fisticuffs.

"Soon," Eddie replied. "I-I promise."

It was all Eddie could do to slip inside the stage doors. *Whew!* This Casanova stuff wasn't as easy as it looked.

As Eddie sat in the auditorium's fourth row watching the other cast members rehearsing, he further contemplated his new role as Jordan View matchmaker.

You know, he mused, *Maria Rainer should fall in love with Captain von Trapp in real life as well as on stage. The butler and the maid should get together—and it's about time Mr. Kasznar tied the knot. Who better than his twenty-year-old assistant, Ann?*

Then there was Monica. Monica deserved someone special. No one in the cast or crew was worthy of her. As she sang "Do, a deer . . ." with the other Von Trapp children, Eddie caught her glancing down at him and smiling.

It occurred to Eddie, this girl might be the only female in the whole school whose infatuation toward him was natural. There was something sacred about that. Monica would be one person the *Manipulator* would never manipulate.

In fact, Eddie decided, *such sincerity should be rewarded.* He called up Monica's brain pattern and stuck the tiny receiver in his ear. As soon as Eddie and Monica finished rehearsing their song, he pulled her aside and asked if she'd like to go out on a date that Friday.

The thought he heard afterwards was, *Oh, Eddie Fanta, you can be such an idiot sometimes.*

Then she replied, "Sure."

Eddie furrowed his brow. *Even when I can hear their thoughts, I still can't understand them.*

Promo pictures had come out in the school newspaper that week. A bold snapshot at the bottom of page two featured Rolf and Leisl. Monica cut it out and wrote her address and phone number on back. Eddie stuck it in his wallet.

After rehearsal, she offered him another ride home. Eddie accepted, but as the two of them were strolling out toward the parking lot, Eddie froze in his tracks. His eyes caught sight of a certain Buick parked in the street—one with an odd-colored passenger door, likely obtained from a local junkyard. Black spraypaint covered some writing on the hood. Inside were Mikey Swearingen and Tanya.

"What's the matter?" asked Monica.

"I gotta go back. I forgot. There's something I gotta do. You go on without me, Monica. I'll talk to you tomorrow."

Eddie pretended to go back into the auditorium, but he stopped on the opposite side of the lobby's glass doors. As soon as Monica's Accord pulled away, Eddie yanked the wave recorder out of his knapsack. He adjusted his aim, careful that only Mikey was in the cross hairs. The Copperhead's brain pattern lit up the monitor window. He fed the information into the *Manipulator*, pulled the lever to the left, and placed the viewfinder's cross hairs on Tanya's blonde head. He pulled the trigger.

Tanya leaped out of the Buick and stomped down the sidewalk. Mikey climbed out as well, demanding to know what the problem was.

Eddie fed his own pattern into the *Manipulator* and zapped Tanya again before she got out of range. Then he threw open the lobby doors and called Tanya's sweet name.

She turned. Their eyes locked. At first she appeared confused, needing a moment to come to grips with this new, grand emotion which engulfed her.

I love that boy, she thought to herself. *I love him more than I've ever loved anyone—more than I thought it was possible to love someone. Yet I don't even remember his name . . . Allen? Danny? Andy? What was it?*

But alas, what did names matter? He was standing there now, calling her to him with an outstretched hand. She began gliding toward the auditorium doors, her legs kicking faster and faster, and when she arrived, the boy opened his arms to receive her embrace. She fell into them (what else could she do?) and went limp with the majesty of his touch. He stole a kiss and she reciprocated. When their lips parted, her eyelashes flickered. She studied the face of her faintly familiar Adonis and with cracking voice asked, "Now . . . what was your name again?"

"Edward," he boldly replied. "Edward Fanta." If he'd had a double 'O' number like a certain member of the British Secret Service, he might have tagged that onto the end as well.

Fifty yards away, in the street by his Buick, Mikey Swearingen was watching. If his teeth had been glass, they'd have shattered all over the street. If his fingernails had been claws, there'd have been puncture holes in the door of his car. And if his eyes had been lasers, the entire school would have exploded in flames.

*　*　*　*

"Is Monica there?"

"This is she."

"Hi Monica. Eddie Fanta here."

"Well, hi, Eddie. I wondered when you'd call—"

"Yeah. Hey, listen. About this Friday. Something's come up."

Silence.

"You see, I was gonna take you to a play downtown. My mom got the tickets from her work. I thought she was just *giving* them to me, see—no strings attached. Turns out, she was expecting we'd go together. Kind of a mother/son thing."

"I see."

"I owe you a big one, okay?"

"Sure. Fine. Thanks for letting me know."

"Hey, no problem. See you at rehearsal."

"Right. See you later."

After the phones hung up, Eddie bit his lower lip. *I don't think she bought it.*

Still in her kitchen, Monica LaRoche became a raging bull. With one sweep of her arm she sent every magnet on the refrigerator soaring across the room. A loaf of bread on the counter became newly unleavened under a dozen strikes from her fists.

She hadn't believed a single word. She'd heard the rumors—how Eddie had stolen Mikey Swearingen's girlfriend. *Heck!* She'd witnessed for herself the bizarre infatuation which every girl in school had suddenly sprouted for him. Even Mr. Kasznar became annoyed Wednesday when seven screaming females snuck into the auditorium to watch Eddie rehearse. "Eddie, will you *please* keep your fan club outside until opening night!" he insisted.

Monica saw her twelve-year-old brother passing by and grabbed his lapels.

"Why?" she screamed in his face. "Why do I let him do this to me? I *know* better! When will I learn?! When *will* I learn!"

She took the chant to bed with her that night.

Eddie felt terrible. He even lifted the receiver to call her back, but before he could dial, his thoughts turned to Tanya. The green-eyed princess had him mesmerized. Her emotions may not have been . . . *un*motivated. But who cared! Every time she peered at him with those emerald peepers, Eddie's feelings of guilt and fraud promptly faded.

It didn't take long for him to peg Tanya as one wild woman. The girl seemed to be living out a death wish! More than once Eddie watched her waltz into moving traffic, forcing cars to swerve or slam on their brakes. It scared Eddie to death, but Tanya laughed hysterically. She owned a little bronze Chevette and though Eddie wasn't Catholic, he was tempted to cross himself every time he climbed inside. For most drivers, a yellow traffic signal was hint enough to stop. Even after a light had turned cherry red, Tanya was still plowing through.

In spite of Tanya's craziness, Eddie wondered if he'd ever felt so free of worldly pressures. It would have been perfect, except for the time he and his conscience had to spend with Louis Kosserinski. His evening readings with the old man became the most grueling exercises in concentration he'd ever endured. He knew if he let his mind slip even once to contemplate something associated with the *Manipulator*, the party was over. He'd think about Tanya, about Duck, about the *Book of Mormon*—about *anything!*—as long as it wasn't the *Manipulator*. He discovered that trying *not* to think about something was brutally difficult. Whenever Eddie felt his thoughts slipping, he'd internally repeat the lyrics of George Harrison's song "I Got My Mind Set On You." Eddie could only hope Louis wouldn't discover the missing invention on his own.

The next weekend, Eddie's hopes ran out. The crippled old man confronted him the moment he stepped into the study.

"I know you took it," he began, "so your brain can stop droning that asinine song."

"I only borrowed it," Eddie defended. "If you knew why, you'd understand."

"I *know* why," Louis proclaimed.

Of course he knew. How silly to think he didn't. Eddie had dropped all defenses. His mind was an open book.

Louis expounded, "You wanted to reunite your family when you visit your father over Thanksgiving. You actually believe such a phenomenon might restore something *natural*."

"It *is* nat—"

Louis rolled forward, "You also believe this will bring peace to yourself! Well, you're wrong!"

Louis was so intense his grisly features resonated in Eddie the horror he felt when they first met.

"I'm not wrong!" Eddie clamored. "Don't you see? You were right when you said it was me I needed to forgive."

Eddie's thoughts kept spilling out like milk from an over-turned bucket. Louis recited them as he heard them. "You think it's all your fault," he stated. "You believe you killed your grandfather."

"I *did* kill him!" Eddie cried. "He told me he was tired. He told me to come back later. I wouldn't go! I kept egging him on! Grandpa just . . . he just slumped over. And that's when it all started. The bitterness. The yelling—"

"The *Manipulator* won't help you. If anything, it will destroy you."

The boy scoffed. "You don't understand your own invention. Why did you build it if you didn't want it to end sadness and misery in the world?"

"The *Manipulator* was merely the culmination of several areas of experimentation. I *never* intended to release it. I have no desire to end sadness in the world."

"But you told me the jacket was supposed to end all fear. You can end fear but not sadness?"

"That's right!" Louis snapped. "The jacket abolishes fear. The *Translator* abolishes ignorance. Such characteristics are not of God. But sadness *is* of God! Even God feels sorrow. Sorrow builds. Sorrow inspires. Sorrow makes us stronger."

Eddie shook his head. His attempt to use Louis's warped sense of logic against him had backfired. He believed this logic only because it justified his own life. At last, after all this time, Eddie finally had to start accepting the truth about Louis. He *is* crazy, Eddie thought.

"Crazy, am I?" Louis ranted. "Crazy because I have the ability to pick and choose what gifts I give the world?"

"No. Crazy because you think I'm gonna deliver any of them for you. If you really think these things can better the world, why don't you sell them to a factory?"

"Because these are tools of godhood. God does not work through lucre-hungry corporations and retail outlets. He works through men—usually young men who can be molded and groomed for his purposes. Men like ancient Mormon. Men like Joseph Smith. But not men like Edward Fanta. You've failed your mission! I want the *Manipulator* back! I want *all* my inventions back!"

"I can't!" Eddie cried. "I *need* the *Manipulator*."

"It's a tool for cowards, Edward! Cowards who can't shape their own destinies! Are you a coward, Edward Fanta?"

The hair pricked on the back of Eddie's neck. "How can you sit there and tell me about cowards? How long has it been since you've stepped even one inch out of this yard? You think you can help the world? You don't even remember who lives in it! You've been in that cellar of yours, hiding—*cowering!*—for forty years, terrified because out there you might not be able to manipulate and control everybody as easily as you do me!"

"I've never manipulated you," defended Louis, "except to call you to my home."

"Oh no?" Eddie stepped over to the space in the bookshelf with the paper folded animals and scattered them with a sweep of his hand. "What about this? It's all a lie! You stole it from my head!"

Louis heart suddenly constricted. He'd been unmasked. His voice cracked. "I did it for your sake, Edward."

Eddie lowered his voice, though to Louis it resonated like thunder. "You did it for yours. *You* know it and *I* know it. That's the ability you gave me."

Eddie's hand rested on the *Translator* which hung on his belt—the same one he'd fed Louis's brain pattern into for the past four nights as a kind of self-defense in case Louis began reading his secrets. Louis had certainly seen it there, but he'd never feared he might be betrayed by his own thoughts. The old man was speechless.

"I'm not a thief," Eddie said finally. "To prove it, I'll bring back the jacket. But I need the *Translator* and I need the *Manipulator* . . . just for awhile."

Eddie turned and left. Louis remained in the dim light of his study for another full hour. He was angry, but not at Eddie. He was angry because his eyes could no longer shed tears.

• *TEN* •

The late-night flights were the cheapest. Eddie's dad had the seat booked three months in advance, making it cheaper still. At the Salt Lake International Airport, Eddie's mother handed him his ticket and delivered an uncharacteristic kiss to his cheek. She'd been a nervous wreck all day. Her mood drove Eddie nuts. *Does she think I'm never coming back? That Dad's gonna kidnap me and flee the country? Give me a break!*

Eddie's only carryon as he entered the concourse was his knapsack. His intentions were to return with much more.

As the plane left the runway, Eddie's thoughts turned to Louis. It had been over a week since he'd seen him. He'd placed the old man's usual list of groceries and accessories on his porch that afternoon, but he worried nonetheless.

As promised, Eddie returned the jacket. He'd wanted to sneak it into Louis's cellar and hang it back in the cabinet, but when he tried, Eddie found the cellar door locked for the first time. Out of spite, Eddie tossed it over an old dusty monitor shell on Louis's porch.

Eddie sighed. *Why should I worry? He was only using me!* Louis was just a warped old man. Once Eddie's parents were reunited in marriage, the void which had drawn him to Louis might not even exist anymore.

The stewardess was slow getting Eddie a *7-Up* so he used the *Manipulator* on her and received considerably better service. As he deplaned in Las Vegas, he zapped her back to normal. Eddie had no intention of leaving a broken heart in every port. After all, he had scruples.

Dad, Michelle, and the Swamp Things had all gathered to meet him at McCarran Airport. They'd even drawn up a banner which read, *Welcome to Las Vegas, Eddie!* Michelle gave Eddie a kiss and hug as if she'd known him all his life, as if she could lay claim to her role as stepmother without asking his permission. The eight-year-old boy, Jesse, offered to carry his knapsack. Eddie refused. Jesse looked grateful. Dad must have coerced him into making the offer beforehand.

"We have a great weekend planned for you, son," his father boasted.

"Tomorrow night we'll show you the lights of the strip," Michelle continued.

"And the Las Vegas Temple," Dad added.

Eddie looked at his father queerly. *Dad wants to show me an LDS temple?*

"We've planned the biggest Thanksgiving spread you've ever seen," his dad declared. "Even bigger than the one your mother's aunt prepared two years ago."

Eddie frowned. Did Dad intend to spend the whole weekend topping everything their family had ever done together? Eddie's resolve to zap him grew firmer.

Dad led them through the parking garage, stopping at the foot of a glistening black limousine.

"Here we are," he announced.

"You're kidding!?" Eddie's reaction was exactly as everyone had hoped. The boy had never seen a back seat so spacious, like a dining room! It could have seated half the United States Senate. There was even a television!

So this was his dad's new job in the "city that never sleeps," a driver and dispatch manager for a local limousine service.

"Way to go, Dad!" Eddie congratulated.

"Take a look at this." His father reached into the glove box and produced a tiny leather-bound book with the word "Autographs" engraved in gold on the cover.

Eddie looked over his father's collection: Don Rickles, Tammy Wynette, Milton Berle, and Jimmy Walker.

"Do you ever drive anybody from *my* generation?" asked Eddie.

"Well, I drove Prince. You heard of him?"

"Sure!"

"But he wouldn't give me his autograph. Some people are like that. You have to be careful in the limo business. Folks sometimes don't like a driver who acts like a groupie. Then again, just today one of my drivers got Tom Talon's autograph. Mr. Talon actually *offered* it."

"Tom Talon is here?"

"He's staying at *Caesar's*. You a fan of his?"

"A girl I know is."

"A girlfriend?"

"Monica? No, she's just a friend." *A friend to whom I owe a big favor,* Eddie recalled.

*   *   *   *

It *was* a big spread, both a turkey *and* a ham on account of Michelle's children hating one or the other. No wonder they were spoiled brats.

Eddie was forced to view all the pictures from Michelle and Dad's June wedding. It was a quiet affair conducted by Michelle's bishop in a local Mormon church. His dad, in the rented black tuxedo, looked sincerely happy. So much so it made Eddie uncomfortable. *If he thinks this'll foil my plan, he's sadly mistaken.*

The next day, Dad and Michelle drove him around the Las Vegas Temple. Michelle leaned on Dad's shoulder and spoke of a day in the "not-too-distant" future when they could be married here for time and all eternity. Eddie's blood started boiling. *My dad was* already *married in the temple.*

Eddie still harbored many questions about his parents' divorce. Though Eddie blamed much on himself, he never really understood what had happened to make Dad leave that day. The couple went out to eat and his father never returned. Mrs. Fanta came home and announced they were "quitting the marriage." How Eddie hated her that night! She'd said it so casually. The boy feared he'd go his entire life without knowing the facts. Tomorrow was his last chance for answers.

Dad had to work Saturday afternoon. The first client was a regular who flew in from San Jose every other weekend to gamble at the *Flamingo Hilton*. Mr. Fanta let Eddie tag along in the passenger's seat. Before leaving the house, Eddie punched up the four-letter code for his mother's brain wave pattern and fed it into the *Manipulator* gun.

When they picked up Dad's client, the man was slightly inebriated. Too many little bottles on the flight. Nevertheless, he took great interest in the *Manipulator* and wave recorder on Eddie's lap.

"Whatcha got there, boy?" the man wondered.

"Some stuff I built in school," Eddie replied.

"In school? I've never seen anything like it. What's it do?"

"Actually, it doesn't do anything. It's just supposed to look fancy."

"Let me see that thing!" the man insisted.

Eddie looked to his dad, pleading for help.

"Go on," urged his father. "He won't hurt anything."

What do you mean? The man is falling all over himself!

Reluctantly, Eddie handed the *Manipulator* over the seat. The man took it. As he leaned back he made an awful gurgling sound in his throat. After gliding his fingers along every inch and peering through the viewfinder, he concluded, "I've been in the electronics business for twenty years. There's no way you could have built this. In school? Come on! You're lying, son. This thing's a computer! My best engineer couldn't compact something like this!"

Eddie was terrified that he'd press the trigger. That's all he needed—some bum on Las Vegas Boulevard falling in love with his mother. Eddie reached back and yanked it out of his hands. Because of his condition, the man gave little resistance.

But he kept on ranting. "In school, indeed! Whered'ju get that?" He spoke to Eddie's father. "He's pulling our legs! There's no *way* he could've built that thing."

Reaching into his wallet, the man pulled out a clump of bills. "I'll buy it from you, son. How much you want? Huh? How much you want for that thing?"

"We're here!" Mr. Fanta announced, pulling into the tight circular drive of the *Flamingo Hilton.*

The man was leaning over the seat. "Hold on!" he cried to Mr. Fanta, curling Eddie's nose hairs with his breath. "I'm trying to make a business deal!"

"It's not for sale!" Eddie insisted, leaning forward to protect the *Manipulator* and the rest of his gear from the man's grabby fingers.

"You need some coffee, Mr. Donaldson." Eddie's father helped the man out of the limousine and into the *Flamingo* lobby. All the way he rambled out more offers. His dad got rid of him by saying, "We'll give you a call."

Eddie glanced across the street. There before his eyes were the fountains and statues and *Omnimax* dome of *Ceasar's Palace.* Somewhere in that massive casino resort lurked the illustrious movie star, Tom Talon.

Mr. Fanta hopped back in the car, aiming it toward the freeway. He apologized to Eddie profusely. "They get like that sometimes. Don't worry about it. He'll get drunker as the evening progresses. In the morning, he won't remember a thing. Did he hurt your gizmo?"

"I don't think so."

"You should feel complimented. Mr. Donaldson's the CEO of one of those computer outfits in Silicon Valley."

Eddie wasted no more time. He punched in the code for his father's brain pattern and fed it into the *Translator.* The inner thoughts of Eddie's dad began sounding in his earpiece loud and clear.

"Dad," Eddie began, "what made you leave that day?"

Mr. Fanta smiled warmly, "I guess you *would* have a lot of questions about those events. It must have been pretty hard on you, eh?"

Eddie was insulted he could trivialize it so.

His dad leaned back, "Your mother made a lot of mistakes, Eddie."

Eddie heard the words which fell off his father's lips easily enough, but the words which came through the receiver were slightly altered: *I made a lot of mistakes, Eddie.*

His father continued, "Your mother and I were never happy. Not really."

That was a lie. Eddie didn't need the *Translator* to tell him that.

"You see, your mother's mother died when she was just a little girl. As a result, she sort of idolized her father—your Grandpa Paxton. In your mom's eyes, I could never quite match up to him. I thought when he died things would finally change." Dad shook his head. "They only got worse."

At the same time, Eddie heard: *She couldn't give me everything I needed. I became so desperately bored. I'd been seeing other women for three years. She found out.*

His voice went on: "It's much better this way, Eddie. It just wasn't working. I blame myself as much as her."

You've got to be kidding! The boy felt like his soul had been crumpled into a tiny wad. The ghastly reaction on Eddie's face was inspired by the thoughts, not the words.

Mr. Fanta looked surprised. "Is something the matter?"

What a question! His dad had bold-faced lied! *My dad is a snake! My dad is sewer slime! No wonder my mother is afraid of her own shadow. Over the years, my father must have squeezed every drop of confidence out of her like a grapefruit. And he has the nerve to make his son believe she was at fault!*

"I *love* Michelle," Mr. Fanta proclaimed. "I'm trying to start over and do it right this time."

His father's thoughts confirmed what he was saying, but an extra mentation was added: *Michelle's dreams about a temple marriage are still very, very distant. Even she doesn't know the whole story.*

As the limousine entered the exit ramp at Charleston Boulevard, a pair of tears popped from Eddie's eyes. Prior to this moment, the only resentment he'd harbored toward his father came from the fact that he never sought custody. *No wonder!*

Eddie remembered his mother's face the day she told him the divorce was final. *My bitterness must have hurt her horribly.*

But in spite of it, she'd never down-talked Eddie's father once. *I've been such a jerk. Such a complete jerk.*

Eddie's father noticed the streams on either side of his son's cheeks. Heavy emotion intimidated him. Perhaps he sensed Eddie hadn't believed him, but he made no effort to continue a defense. Instead, he ignored the tears. That was his way. He'd had years of practice with Eddie's mother.

The limousine pulled up in front of the house. Finding the curb, Dad stopped the vehicle and waited for Eddie to climb out. The next client he was scheduled to pick up was new and might not take kindly to the presence of the driver's son.

"Here we are, sport. Tell Michelle I should be home around seven. And no tying Jesse to the piano leg again, okay?"

Mr. Fanta hoped he'd raise a smile, but Eddie only nodded and gathered up his gear. Mr. Fanta was fully aware of the awkwardness between them, but he was unwilling to acknowledge it. As he opened the door, Eddie at last faced his father, aiming the *Manipulator*, which still contained his mother's brain pattern right between the man's eyes.

"Smile big, Dad," Eddie said, struggling to subdue a bite in his voice.

The boy's motivation for doing this was different now. It wasn't to regain a father or to restore a family. It was to punish a criminal. If Dad was, indeed, as happy as he claimed, this would throw a deserved wrench in the machinery of his mind. Eddie depressed the trigger. He watched the smile fade from his father's face, then he headed up the sidewalk. Eddie watched through the window as Mr. Fanta drove away. Though the man was even now being tormented by the revelation that he still loved Eddie's mother, Eddie himself secretly imagined that his real father might have died before he was born and that his mother had covered up the truth all these years. Whether it happened that way or not, such might be the story Eddie would tell people for the rest of his life.

* * * *

Michelle never did the dishes before serving dinner. Never! Tonight she was frustrated and felt she needed to scrub a few pans. She'd been putting her best foot forward, doing everything she could to earn her stepson's acceptance. All she got in return was indifference. Her daughter, Brenda, said he was stuck-up and her son, Jesse, was still determined to get even for being tied to the piano leg.

Michelle tried to empathize—new family, new mother—all that stuff. Even so, her patience was running thin. Also running thin was the teflon coating on the pan she continued to scrub long after it was clean.

As she placed the pan in the dish rack, a car honked outside. The front door opened and closed. *Strange,* she thought. Wiping her hands with a towel, she wandered into the living room to glance through the curtain just in time to see Eddie climbing into a yellow cab!

Dropping the wet towel on the couch, she raced for the door. As her head leaned out, the cab skirted down the street. She shouted Eddie's name, but he was already well out of range.

So that's who he was talking to on the phone! A darn cab company! But how could she begin to guess where he was headed? Turning back into the house, her hands flew over her head.

"That's it!" she ranted. "*I give up!*"

* * * *

The cabby wanted six dollars and forty cents for a fifteen minute jaunt to the Las Vegas Strip. Eddie handed him a five and two ones. The cabby shot into the street without offering change. Eddie frowned. *Maybe I should have studied the bus schedule a little closer.* If this mission proved unsuccessful, it would be a serious waste of the twenty-dollar allowance his mother had given him.

Eddie turned around and faced the light-spangled fortress of Caesar's Palace. He followed some tourists into a pseudo-Roman shrine with a tunnel leading past a holographic mural of toga-clad Romans. A loudspeaker welcomed Eddie to gambling paradise. Eddie hopped onto a moving beltway, clutching his knapsack close to his chest.

The beltway deposited Eddie onto the casino's upper deck. He leaned on the railing, studying the sea of slot machines and blackjack tables. How could Eddie possibly find a movie star like Tom Talon in a place of this size? The Thanksgiving holiday had made Caesar's standing room only.

As Eddie crossed the casino floor, a security guard eyed him suspiciously. Eddie scooted into a marble-floored hallway and past a menagerie of exclusive shops. He blushed when a giggling couple caught him staring at the scantily clad mannequins. The people in this town gave Eddie the creeps. Why couldn't Mr. Talon make this easy and step around the next corner?

Eddie found some elevators. One was open and waiting. He hopped aboard. Certainly a star like Tom Talon would stay in the penthouse. He tried to hit the top-most button, but it wouldn't stay lit. The top floor was off-limits. *Figures.* How silly to think he might simply knock on Tom Talon's door. Eddie hit the second highest button. The elevator lurched upward.

It opened into an empty foyer. Eddie was a single floor below his destination. There had to be a stairway or a fire escape. At the end of a hallway, Eddie found what he wanted: a stairwell leading up. Eddie Fanta ascended.

At the top was a door with a warning: "Roof Access Restricted. Opening Door Will Sound Alarm." *Ah, c'mon,* Eddie scoffed. *They just say that to scare people off.* He turned the knob and pushed.

A horrible screech echoed through the stairwell, as if an ostrich was dying! Plugging his ears, Eddie bounded back toward the elevators. *Maybe Monica would be happy enough with the affections of the governor of Utah or every member of the Utah Jazz.*

Eddie called the elevator again. When it opened, a pair of square-jawed security guards were glowering down.

"What are you doing, kid? What's your room number?"

Eddie stuttered for a second, then bolted down the hallway. The guards barked a threat and took up pursuit. Eddie slipped into the stairwell. Only one guard descended after him. The other climbed to the top to silence the alarm. Three floors below, Eddie popped back into the hallway, racing toward the elevators. As he hit the call button, the guard was just emerging from the stairwell.

The elevator arrived. Eddie leaped aboard. "C'mon kid! Gimme a break!" panted the guard as the elevator door closed.

Eddie chanted, *Just let me get out the front doors. I promise I'll never come back. I promise, I promise, I promise.*

Eddie stepped off on the third floor, fearing a posse of security guards with nets and ropes awaited him in the bottom foyer. He descended the final flights on foot and emerged in the casino. The doors leading to freedom were in sight. As Eddie passed the *Megabucks* slot island a gargantuan hand caught his collar. Struggling was futile. The black guard's rippling muscles were barely contained by his uniform.

"What did I do?" Eddie innocently inquired.

"Give it up, kid. Are you trying to give us grey hair before our time?"

"You got the wrong guy!" the boy insisted.

Sighing, the guard detached the radio from his belt and called up a guard on the other end. "Carl, describe the kid again."

"*Blonde,*" a voice replied. "*'Bout five-eight. Blue jeans, red shirt, light blue knapsack over his shoulder.*"

The guard turned back to Eddie, "Now how many kids in here you think fit that description?"

Eddie shrugged and fidgeted. He was meat loaf.

The man spoke into the radio again. "Got 'im. Disaster averted." Hanging the radio back on his belt, he inquired, "Where ya from, boy?"

"Salt Lake. But my dad lives here. In Las Vegas, I mean."

"We don't restrict roof access 'cause we're bad guys. We do it for safety. What'd you wanna see up there?"

"I was just trying to catch a glimpse of Tom Talon. I'm really sorry."

"Tom Talon! You put us through this to meet Tom Talon?"

"I thought he might be staying in the penthouse."

"The penthouse is for kings and presidents—not movie stars. Mr. Talon is staying in a suite."

"I swear I won't bother you anymore. Please don't arrest me."

The security guard smiled. "Tell ya what. If I show you where Mr. Talon is at this moment, will ya get his autograph and scoot on home to your daddy?"

Was this guy for real?

"You better believe it!" Eddie agreed.

The security guard led the way. "Last I saw, Mr. Talon and his guests were having drinks on *Cleopatra's Barge.*"

It was too good to be true. This *had* to be a ploy. Eddie was being led to a dungeon for sure.

"We see 'celebs' all the time at Caesar's," the guard revealed. "They like Vegas. Don't stand out so much."

Eddie and the guard approached a replica of an ancient Roman ship, the bow of which jutted out into the walkway. On the ship's deck stood tables. Among the patrons, Tom Talon was not. The guard called to a bartender, "Hey Freddy, what happened to Mr. Talon and company?"

"Left a few minutes ago," Freddy called back. "I think they was headed out. Might still catch 'em outside."

The bartender indicated the direction. Without waiting for an escort, Eddie dashed off toward the valet entrance. A crowd had gathered. Only a movie star could attract such a mob. The guard had been wrong. Even in Vegas, Tom Talon couldn't retain anonymity.

Eddie went outside and dropped the knapsack off his shoulder. He pulled out the *Manipulator* with the attached recording unit and pressed the four-letter code calling up Monica's brain pattern. The information fed into the

Manipulator gun. Eddie mined a hole through the crowd. Shortly, he could see snatches of a white limousine, newer and larger than the one his father drove.

There he was, beside the open rear door—Mr. Tom Talon himself—the man whose raven-black hair and icy-blue eyes had lit up more magazine covers in the last year than any other celebrity, especially since a movie he'd starred in took Best Picture in April. Tom, himself, had been snubbed by the Academy. Not even a nomination. Too young, too handsome, hadn't paid enough dues. He was vigorously signing autographs on anything thrust in his face, sporting the same grin which had sold nearly a billion dollars in theater tickets. The movie star was shorter than Eddie expected.

Leaning out of the limousine to tug Mr. Talon's sleeve was a slender redhead with long frizzy hair. "We've got to go," she crooned.

"Okay, baby." Tom Talon turned back to the crowd. "Only two more autographs!"

The crowd was disappointed, but it was that announcement which caused them to break up enough for Eddie to get a clear view of the actor's torso. Eddie hoisted the *Manipulator* to his eye and pulled the trigger.

Mr. Talon didn't react at all. It may be that he now loved Monica LaRoche, but how would he know who she was? And then Eddie remembered the newspaper clipping in his wallet—the one from the play on which Monica had scribbled her address. He pulled it out and held it aloft.

"Mr. Talon!" Eddie shouted.

His shout was ignored. Tom Talon was slipping into the limousine.

"Mr. Talon!"

Eddie pried through the crowd with claustrophobic earnestness, barely reaching the limousine door before the driver slammed it on his arm.

"This is for you!" Eddie called into the darkened vehicle.

The actor's hand reached up to grab the clipping at the same time the driver's hand nabbed Eddie's shoulder.

"That's all for today!" blustered the driver. He closed the

door. The windows were tinted so Eddie couldn't tell if Mr.
Talon had unfolded the clipping or not as the limo pulled
away. But the chances were good. They were very, very
good. *Well,* Eddie thought to himself, wiping a few beads of
sweat from his forehead. *I hope she appreciates this. At
Christmas, Monica LaRoche might have a slightly more nifty
stocking stuffer than she's had in years.*

*   *   *   *

Far away from movie stars and Las Vegas glitter, Louis
Kosserinski awoke at an unusually early hour. He'd had that
dream again. The one where Eddie Fanta kept ranting the
words, "You think you can help the world? You don't even
remember who lives in it! You've been in that cellar of
yours, hiding—*cowering!*—for forty years!" Only tonight,
Eddie's face had changed to the face of his wife, and then to
the face of his son. Louis looked at the clock. It was 4:30 A.M.
Four-and-a-half hours before the meeting began.

During the first hour he completed his routine of exercise
and bathing. Thirty years before, the same routine had taken
three times as long, but he'd constructed many helpful
appliances since then, including an apparatus which lifted
him in and out of the bath basin. It took another hour to dig
up his charcoal-grey *Brooks Brothers* suit, circa 1950, and
attach it to the dressing machine. Over it, he awkwardly
wore the red hooded sweat jacket. Ninety minutes were
required for him to assemble the electric wheelchair. He
didn't like to use it much, but the chapel was nearly a mile
away. He'd need the last hour simply to go the distance.

A protein and vitamin drink coupled with a slice of home-
made bread comprised his breakfast. After painstakingly
laying out the proper ramps, he lowered himself onto the
front walk.

The air was stiff. He could see his breath float up like
steam from a teapot. When his wheelchair reached the iron
gate, Louis paused. It had been—a decade?—maybe longer
since he'd ventured even this far. He glanced back. Behind

him now were all the riggings and pulleys, buttons and mechanisms, which made his life secure. Beyond the gate was . . . uncertainty; shadows cast from unknown sources, loud sounds, unpredictable movement.

He grasped the cold steel picket. The horrible squeak of the hinges had once signified to Eddie and Duck passage into a haunted realm. To Louis it signified passage into a haunted world.

The neighborhood was not so different, though he remembered the tiny homes across the street were once clean and unpeeling. He began the three-quarter mile trek. Cars obliviously whizzed by. So many new designs. Yet, Louis was disappointed. Why couldn't the auto industry seem to develop an engine which converted carbon-monoxide wastes into a useful bi-product?

A ten-year-old girl who'd been riding up and down the walk in front of her home gasped when she saw him and dropped her bicycle. As the girl scurried inside, Louis mentally transformed himself again. His body was perfect. Nevertheless, Louis pulled the hood strings on his sweat jacket, shrouding his face a little more.

At last the chapel spires loomed overhead. Louis had never seen the new building, though a contribution he'd made nearly fifteen years before had paid for much of its construction. For the first time in over thirty-nine years, Louis Kosserinski wheeled himself inside a chapel of God. The meeting hadn't yet begun. Brothers were shaking hands. Sisters were chatting. When Louis entered, everyone's voice became a whisper. After a moment, children were scolded and told to turn forward.

While strolling past Louis on his way to the pulpit, the bishop habitually offered his hand. Timidly, Louis raised a disfigured limb. The leader hesitated. When Louis finally received the bishop's shake, he held on. Contact with living flesh rushed into him like warm liquid. Nerve endings he'd thought were long since shriveled ignited to life.

"I'm Brother Kosserinski," Louis said softly.

"Welcome," replied the bishop uncertainly. He retrieved

his hand, nodded, and took his seat on the stand. As the meeting began, the leader thought perhaps he should have said something more.

As the sacrament was passed, Louis observed a little girl two pews ahead. She was no more than eighteen months old, grinning shyly at him over her mother's shoulder. Louis tried to smile back, but her mother innocently took the infant into her arms, hiding her from view. Louis smiled anyway. He smiled for a long time.

For a brief moment, his mind seemed to drift out of an angry and turbulent storm into a hurricane's eye. Everything seemed suddenly clear. His mind was lucid, perhaps more so than ever before in his life. *Thank God for Eddie Fanta. Thank God I came to this place.* For the gift of Christ's sacrament and a little girl's grin, he'd have gladly wheeled here by hand the entire night.

• *ELEVEN* •

Looking out the window, it seemed to Eddie the number of lights between Las Vegas and Salt Lake could be counted on a single hand. It was one A.M. when the airplane touched down at Salt Lake's airport. Though Eddie had tried to sleep, the business yuppie beside him insisted on keeping the reading light glaring.

But the light wasn't the only thing keeping him awake. Eddie kept mulling over the last thing his father had said.

"I'll follow you home in a couple days," he promised. "I wouldn't miss your play for the world."

Michelle was clearly shocked. "But honey, we've talked about this. Remember? We have plans that week."

"It's my son's play!" Mr. Fanta insisted. "What kind of father would I be if I missed it?"

Michelle's smile was painted on the rest of the time. As soon as Eddie disappeared down the concourse, he could bet sparks had flown. But Eddie knew his dad was too determined to change his mind. Only Eddie knew why. Eddie's vengeful attitude had simmered a bit. His father was slime, but he *was* still his father. Eddie hoped the *Manipulator* had actually excised what was vile about his dad's personality and restored some sense of virtue.

His mother was late. Eddie remained in the gate area, seating himself in a chair which faced the other end of the wing. At this hour, the airport was practically empty. Eddie would see his mother coming from quite some distance. He pulled the *Manipulator* out of his knapsack, punched up the code for his father's brain pattern and balanced the unit on his lap.

A moment later his mother appeared, her long coat and brown hair bouncing as she rushed past the other gates. She wasn't wearing a drop of makeup. Even from this distance, Eddie could see the dark circles under her eyes. She'd obviously tried to sleep a few hours before meeting the plane. Still, Eddie wondered if he'd ever seen such a pretty lady. Michelle would never look so good at her age.

Mrs. Fanta smiled and waved. Eddie brought the *Manipulator* to his eye and pulled the trigger.

When he lowered the unit, Mrs. Fanta wasn't moving toward him as swiftly. Her expression had changed. She looked remarkably sullen, perplexed. Then she stopped walking altogether.

Eddie arose and went to her.

As they embraced, the first question out of his mother's mouth was, "How's your father?"

"I thought you might ask something like that," Eddie replied.

*   *   *   *

It was Monica's turn to present the lesson in family home evening that night. She wasn't in the best of moods for such an assignment. All day in school she'd had to listen to girls in the hallway crooning about the school's new stud machine, Eddie Fanta. There were at least fifty—no exaggeration—*fifty* girls thronging the auditorium doors when play rehearsal let out on Monday, all hoping to catch a glimpse. At the head of the pack was that sleeze-bucket Tanya.

Monica was convinced something was seriously wrong. As for Eddie, she'd actually begun to *loathe* the little creep. Certainly a portion of her resentment was sour grapes, but . . . no, it was more than that. Eddie Fanta had *changed*. He wasn't the same person he'd been only a month before.

On stage that night, when Eddie leaned forward to kiss her, Monica inserted her palm between their mouths. Mr. Kasznar was so amused he let it pass. Afterwards, Eddie stopped her backstage to ask why.

Monica laid into him with, "I'm not one of your simpering groupies, Eddie, and I'm not going to be treated like one. I kiss you on stage because it's my job—not because I like it."

Eddie tried to be understanding. "You're still mad about the date I cancelled, aren't you?"

Monica's face reddened. "Don't flatter yourself. Outside of this play I don't want anything to do with you."

"I hope you won't be mad forever," said Eddie. "Any day now I expect you'll get quite a surprise in the mail. I'd tell you who it's gonna be from, but you'd never believe it."

"What are you talking about?"

"Just part of the favor I owe you."

"What makes you think I want your favors, Eddie Fanta?"

"Nothing, I—"

"What makes you think I want *anything* from you?"

Actors rehearsing on stage had stopped to listen. The director considered stepping backstage to foil the bloodshed. Monica left rehearsal early, warning everyone to keep back as she stormed out the stage doors.

During dinner, Mrs. LaRoche tried to learn the cause of her daughter's distress, but Monica was silent. Her father offered to teach the home evening lesson, but Monica insisted. Faltering in her family obligations somehow meant Eddie Fanta was winning. Any suggestion of victory on his part was something she'd beat down to her last breath.

Nevertheless, she couldn't bring herself to look at the home evening manual until five minutes beforehand. The topic was improving communication skills and controlling one's temper. Monica rolled her eyes. *Puh-leeez. Any night but tonight!* She skimmed through the table of contents for a lesson on "Righteous Indignation."

About the time her family started to gather in the living room, the doorbell rang. Tessa, her five-year-old sister, went to answer it. Monica had a secret feeling it would be Eddie even before Tessa came back and announced: "It's a boy for Monica."

Monica breathed deeply. On the way down the hall she decided if any hint of Tanya's brown Chevette was in the driveway, she'd slam the door in his face. If he was alone and looking wretched, she might be courteous enough to let him choke out a few sentences before doing exactly the same thing.

The hallway to the door wasn't well lit. The porch light hanging at the lip of the roof gave the figure a halo of soft yellow light. Features were difficult to distinguish.

Monica knew immediately it wasn't Eddie. Two day's growth of stubble covered the man's chin and a red sports car—a Ferrari, no less!—was parked in the driveway. The first words from the stranger's lips were, "Monica? You *are* Monica, right? Monica LaRoche?"

The voice was familiar, but it didn't belong to anyone she encountered daily.

"Yes, that's right." In the next instant, she recognized him. Both her hands flew up over her mouth.

"*Oh, my gosh!*" She babbled, "Are you—? You're—! I can't believe—! *Oh, my gosh!*"

He put forth his hand, "My name is Tom Talon."

"*I know who you are!*" Monica screamed. The rest of the family had gathered behind her.

The actor hung there a moment more, at last deciding the girl wasn't coherent enough to shake hands. "Sorry to intrude like this. I was going to call. I just didn't know what to—"He was cut short by Monica's screaming sister, Allison— loud enough to shatter glass.

"Who is he?" Monica's father implored.

"Dad!" raved Monica's brother, Hubert. "Don't you recognize Tom Talon?"

Mrs. LaRoche was the one who finally invited him inside. The actor wore a custom-designed leather coat, faded blue-jeans, and snakeskin cowboy boots. Even without the benefit of makeup or studio lighting, his eyes were as deep blue as the Carribean. Monica followed in silent awe while her mother led her dream-idol to the living room.

"How far have you come?" asked Mrs. LaRoche.

"I left L.A. at 5:30 this morning. Long drive. I haven't taken such a road trip in years."

"Can we get you anything?"

"Sure. I'd love some coffee—cream, no sugar."

"I'm afraid we don't have coffee. How about hot chocolate?"

"Well, okay. If it's not too much trouble."

"Trouble! Are you kidding?" Allison screamed one more time.

Mr. LaRoche gestured for Tom to take a seat. The children continued squealing and giggling. All the while, Tom couldn't keep his eyes off Monica, now seated in the *Lazyboy* at his left.

"So you're a movie star?" asked Monica's father.

The kids were dying inside. *How could Dad ask such imbecile questions?*

"That's right," Tom replied.

"What movies have you been in?"

"Well, did you see *Passion and Thunder*?"

"Was it rated R?"

Tom tried to recall. "I think it was."

"Then I'm afraid I haven't."

Monica's sister grabbed her father's shirt sleeve. "Dad, you're *embarrassing* us!"

Tom was persistent. "How about *Navy Ace*?"

Mr. LaRoche shook his head, "I'm afraid I don't get out to movies much."

"We've only rented it about six hundred times!" cried Hubert. Was it really possible for a person on planet Earth not to recognize Tom Talon?

"So what brings you to Salt Lake?" asked Mr. LaRoche.

Tom glanced up at Monica. "To be honest, I'm not really sure. It's been a confusing weekend. There are a lot of people angry with me at the moment. My agent has likely called 'missing persons' by now. Not to mention . . . well, let's just say I'm not myself lately."

Mr. LaRoche looked more than a bit perplexed. Tom

finally broke down and confessed, "I'm here to see your daughter, Mr. LaRoche. I've come to see Monica."

Every eyebrow in the room shot up. Mrs. LaRoche handed the actor his hot chocolate. Tom thanked her and stole a sip.

"Do you *know* Monica?" asked Mr. LaRoche

"Yes. I mean, no. That is, I *feel* like I know her."

Those deep blue eyes were still riveted on Monica.

She let out a nervous laugh. "I don't understand."

Tom invited, "Maybe we—you and I—could go for a ride or something? Talk for a while?"

There was a pain in his face Monica had never seen in a movie role. "I guess that would be okay," she replied. She looked to her father for confirmation.

He responded, "We're right in the middle of family home evening."

"Daaaad." Monica was stern. "I think under the circumstances . . ."

"Go on, love," her mother consented.

Mr. LaRoche sent his wife a glance which said, *Are you crazy? We don't even know this person!*

"Don't worry, Dad," Monica assured, as if reading his mind. "I'll be fine."

*   *   *   *

The Ferrari's dashboard looked like a spaceship's control panel. The seats were custom leather, hugging snugly at Monica's shoulders. She was still in a daze. Only half an hour before, she'd been preparing a family lesson. Now she was seated beside Hollywood's biggest celebrity, the very face which stared down from the poster on her ceiling. Only now, it was living and breathing.

"I'm sorry," apologized Tom. "I didn't mean to put you on the spot."

"It's no problem, Mr. Talon."

"Call me Tom."

"Okay . . . Tom."

"I just wanted to talk to you."

Monica nodded awkwardly. "Okay."

"To be with you."

Monica turned forward. She stuck her hands in her coat pockets, then on her lap, then back in her coat pockets. "Um, listen, Mr. T—Tom. This whole thing is *really* . . ."

"I know. Strange."

". . . freaking me out! Why in the world would you want to meet *me*?"

Tom turned the ignition. "Maybe we should drive somewhere. I think better when I'm driving."

A low gas gauge forced Mr. Talon to stop at the *Circle K* on the corner. Monica remained in the car while he filled his own tank. Somehow, watching Tom Talon pumping gas made him human. But when he went inside to pay, myth and legend took over again. One of the ladies behind the counter started screaming like Allison. Customers gathered around. Tom found a pen in his jacket, handy for just such occasions, and signed a few napkins and *Thirstbuster* cups. Monica was startled by a lady's face when it pressed against the Ferrari's tinted windows, trying to see who was inside.

"Can I have your autograph?" she called tactlessly through the glass.

Monica found herself signing a coupon book. The lady took it back to her car and announced to a friend, "I got his girlfriend's signature, too!" Monica giggled in disbelief.

Tom hopped back into the Ferrari, having made his escape.

"I knew I should have worn my sunglasses," he said.

"Do you go through this every day, Mr. Talon?" Monica asked.

"Tom."

"Tom," Monica corrected.

"I've learned not to go out in public much."

More fans were approaching the vehicle.

"We better scoot," Tom suggested.

"Where did you want to go?"

"This is your town. You point the way."

They found themselves driving west on Highway 201, out toward the Great Salt Lake.

"You know, my real name is Thomas Antonio Gustavio."

"Really?"

"Yeah. Not too pretty on the big screen. Listen, do you mind if I smoke?" Tom pulled a pack out of his coat.

"Well. To be honest . . ."

Without hesitation, Tom put the pack away.

Monica rolled eyes at herself. "I'm sorry," she said. "That was rude. This is your car—"

"No problem. I'm just a little nervous around you still."

Tom Talon smokes? Monica tried desperately not to feel judgmental, but the news was grossly deflating.

"So you're Mormon then?" Tom observed.

"Yes, though we prefer to be called Latter-day Saints."

"Myself, I'm a Catholic."

"Yeah, I heard that somewhere," Monica admitted. "I heard you once even considered becoming a priest."

Tom grinned, "For about a day. The truth is, I love women—" Looking closer at Monica, he altered his statement. "—that is, I love *girls*—too much."

Monica blushed. The conversation lagged. Awkwardness still prevailed. The Ferrari continued to weave its way through the industrial countryside. Finally, Tom parked in front of the old SaltAir Palace at the edge of the lake, a one time dance hall and tourist site whose mid-east style domes still silhouetted the night. It was all but ruins now, having been destroyed by the flood of '83. A few tourist stands remained though, selling T-shirts and lake momentos and providing the beachfront with a romantic splash of light.

"Would you like to take a walk?" Tom inquired.

"Well, all right," Monica replied, uncertainly.

It was an unusually warm night for the season. Low clouds reflected the lights of nearby Salt Lake City, making it possible to see the shadows of distant hills across the water.

"I'm not like this normally," Tom began as the two of them wandered down a stony road leading to the waterfront. "I've spent six years in my business developing a reputation for being a serious actor. I feel like I'm blowing it all away in one shining moment. My marriage too."

"You're *married*?" Monica shrieked.

"No, no. Engaged," Tom quickly clarified. "Sharon Bettis. She was my co-star in *Naked Fury*."

"I never saw that one." Monica stumbled slightly as her shoe stubbed a stone. Tom caught her with lightning efficiency. It's not as if she would have fallen, but Tom firmly held her hand anyway. Monica felt a shiver. She wasn't sure if the shiver was euphoria or fear.

"Until two days ago, I thought Sharon was the most beautiful creature on two legs," Tom continued. "We moved in together right after the production wrapped."

Monica yanked her hand away. "So, what happened two days ago?"

Tom stopped and grabbed Monica's shoulders, turning her toward him. "I saw your picture, Monica. That's all I know. I've been desperate to meet you ever since. Nothing else has mattered. I know it sounds crazy. *Believe* me, I *know*!"

Monica was speechless—utterly dumbfounded.

"I love you, Monica," Tom proclaimed. "You've become my very reason for breathing. I see your face in everything good in this world. Touching you is the only hope I have of being a part of that goodness. Kissing you is . . . is . . ."

Before Monica knew it, his lips were pressed against hers. Monica's eyes shot up like a window blind. *Wait a second! That was the same corny line he told the Admiral's daughter in Navy Ace!* Monica thrust him back.

"You barely know me! What's the matter with you?"

Tom Talon was stunned. It had been a long time since a woman hadn't simply melted in his arms at will. Confused, he added, "But I *do* know you. Don't you understand? I want you to come back to Los Angeles with me. I don't make offers like this to a girl every day."

He stepped forward.

"Stay back!" Monica searched the ground for a weapon. She found a twig and held it between them. "I'm warning you!"

"But I'm Tom Talon!"

"Tell me where you saw my picture!" Monica demanded.

The actor reached into his pocket and pulled out the clipping. Monica watched him unfold it. She gasped.

"Where did you get that?"

"In Las Vegas. Someone in the crowd handed it to me."

Monica snatched it away and turned it over. Sure enough, there was the address and phone number she'd scribbled two weeks before.

Eddie! A lot of mysteries were coming into focus. *Eddie Fanta is responsible for this!* But how? The prospect of seeking an answer was almost terrifying. But she had no alternative. Monica would confront this mystery with the same zeal she used to confront any other situation. Like a stampeding rhino.

*   *   *   *

When Eddie opened the door, he was greeted by Monica's sour brow. Monica noted the couple on the couch. She assumed the lady was Eddie's mother. Since she was aware of the divorce, she'd have never guessed the man was his father. But it was. Mr. Fanta had driven up from Las Vegas that afternoon, a full week before the *Sound of Music* was set to perform.

"Monica!" Eddie exclaimed. "What a surprise!"

He saw the figure leaning on the sports car at the end of the driveway. Monica had requested Tom to stay back while she talked.

"Who's the guy with the Ferrari?" Eddie whispered.

Monica grabbed Eddie Fanta's lapels and yanked him out the door, pushing him against the side of the house. Eddie's parents were too busy making goo-goo eyes to notice the violence.

"I think you know full well who it is," Monica suggested.

"Is that him?" Eddie asked. "Is that Tom Talon?"

Monica considered wiping the smirk off Eddie's face with her fist, but she was too anxious for answers. "What did you do to him, Eddie? He's not himself, and you know it."

"I didn't do anything to him. Not directly at least."

"I know you're responsible, Eddie. And I know that whatever you used on him, you also used on Tanya and half the girls in school. What was it? Did you feed them some kind of potion? Did you put them under a spell?"

"Nothing like that."

"Then *what*!?"

"It's an invention. Almost no one knows about it. It's purely science. Cross my heart."

"And that makes it okay? What kind of crackpot would invent such a thing? How could you use it and live with yourself? These are human beings, Eddie! You're messing with their heads like they were lab rats. They have lives! Tom Talon has put his whole career at stake."

"I was just trying to add a little spice to your life."

"I have enough spice in my life. I want you to fix what you've broken. Turn him back to the way he was. Can you do it?"

Eddie bit his cheek and glanced at Tom Talon, who was leaning toward them, straining to hear.

"Yeah, I can release him. I can even make him hate you if you like."

"Just make him himself again."

That's gratitude for you, thought Eddie. He slipped into the house and returned with the *Manipulator* and wave recorder, shutting the door behind him. Monica watched in amazement as Eddie punched up her brain pattern and fed it into the gun. He set the lever exactly in the middle. After finding Tom Talon in the cross hairs, he pulled the trigger.

Eddie sent Monica an exaggerated smile, like a circus clown. "There! Is everybody happy again?"

Eddie slipped back into the duplex and shut the door. Monica turned to Tom. The actor was blinking tightly as if he'd just awakened from the weirdest possible dream. Monica watched him for a moment. There stood her idol. Her fantasy. Eddie Fanta had handed him to her on a silver platter. She could hardly resent him for it.

Yet Tom Talon looked different to her now. Vulnerable.

Lost. Almost pathetic. The fantasy had dissipated. Their worlds were so far apart. She'd always known that, but a part of her was ever curious, ever yearning to know what being immersed in his glitter-filled lifestyle would be like. Tonight that yearning had died. Unknowingly, Eddie Fanta had given her a great gift.

As for Tom, the situation was much more bewildering. All of a sudden, he barely recognized this girl. She was just a kid! What in blazes had he been thinking?

Timidly, Monica approached the movie star. "I guess," she observed, "that you'll be wanting to get back to Los Angeles."

"Yes," Tom replied.

Monica smiled warmly. "Could you take me home first, Mr. Talon?"

"Yes." Looking into her eyes, Tom sent her another million-dollar grin. As before, he didn't charge her a single penny.

*   *   *   *

"Well?" demanded Mikey Swearingen, nervously puffing one last drag off his cigarette and tossing it out the Buick's window. "What did you find out?"

Miguel needed a second to catch his breath. Mikey didn't normally bother to slow down when fellow gangsters were leaping into his car, whether fleeing a crime scene or not.

"Nothing," Miguel panted. "He always carries a knapsack with cameras and recorders. Maybe the girls are flattered to have their pictures taken."

Mikey swore. "Don't be an idiot. Our friend Eddie Fanta is hiding something. Something big. I'm gonna find out what it is. I don't care what it takes."

"Are you sure you're not makin' all this up to cover for what happened to your car, and what happened to your eye, and what happened to your girl?"

Mikey screeched the Buick to a halt in the middle of the block. A car behind them honked and swerved around. Mikey grabbed Miguel's collar.

"You think I'm makin' this up? You think I've had you tailin' this little maggot for the last three weeks for your health?"

Miguel tore Mikey's fingers off his coat. "Chill out, man! I'm just sayin' there ain't no evidence to prove all this paranoid mumbo-jumbo."

Mikey tried to relax. Miguel had a point.

"Maybe we're not talkin' to the right people," the Copperhead leader suggested.

"Maybe not. Who you got in mind?"

Mikey reached into his jacket for another cigarette. As he flicked his lighter, he replied, "Don't worry. I got a pretty good idea who'll tell us what we want to know—that is, if we offer 'em plenty of the right kind of encouragement . . ."

• *TWELVE* •

Once again, Eddie was rudely awakened by the front door-bell. His mother called for him to get up and answer it, as she was finishing getting dressed. Bleary-eyed, Eddie staggered to the door wondering how anyone could be expected to function on only nine hours sleep. He expected it to be his father. The family had planned a Sunday picnic at two. To his shock, it was his Heckle-and-Jeckle home teachers, Brother Schlyter and Brother Hurst. Eddie had thought he'd never see these guys again. It wouldn't have surprised him to learn that one had moved out of the neighborhood to get away from the other.

"May we come in?" asked Brother Schlyter.

"Uh, well . . ."

"It'll only take a minute," pleaded Brother Hurst.

"Come on in," Eddie agreed, reluctantly.

Mrs. Fanta emerged from the bedroom, pinning on an earring. "We wanted you both to know," began Brother Schlyter, "we feel quite embarrassed for the way we behaved last month. It was an odd day for both of us."

"We've spent much time on bended knee since then—fasting too," continued Brother Hurst. "We wanted to apologize and let you both know we sincerely care about your family."

"Thank you," said Eddie's mother. "We actually enjoyed your last visit. Glad to have you back."

Without further delay, the home teachers proceeded with a specially prepared lesson on tolerance.

These guys are incredible! thought Eddie. Not an ounce of animosity between them. *How much abuse do they think they can take?*

"Excuse me," Eddie interrupted. "Gotta make some adjustments on my school project."

Eddie grabbed the *Manipulator*. For the second time, he zapped each of them with high levels of enmity—toward himself, toward his mother, and toward each other.

They continued the lesson unflustered. What was the problem? Eddie checked the connections. The brain patterns were recalled easily enough. The indicators in the viewfinder were operating fine. The feed line was registering. *Why isn't it working?*

Either something was internally wrong or else—it was almost too startling to consider—their brains had become immune! At least immune to Eddie's previous manipulations. The exertion necessary to untie such mental knots would have been remarkable. It was impossible! Wasn't it?

Eddie wondered if he ought to zap his favorite victims, Tanya for instance, a second time—just to be safe.

* * * *

Come Tuesday evening, Jordan View High School's auditorium was alive with the *Sound of Music*. Long before the curtains opened, ticket sellers were turning people away in droves. Over two hundred girls were now "Fanta-stricken." Most of the girls were students at Jordan View, but Eddie hadn't been particular. Many were from the highways and byways of Salt Lake County—whichever gorgeous females happened to be crossing the street while Eddie rode by with his finger on the trigger. Eddie wasn't sure why he zapped so many. Part ego? Part revenge? Mostly, it was just doggone fun.

The only girl who didn't show up tonight was Tanya. Eddie peeked through the curtain to see if she was sitting in her designated front-row seat. How could she miss opening night? Her place was still empty when the orchestra trumpeted the opening bars of Act One, Scene One.

When Eddie Fanta stepped on stage in Scene Six, the auditorium was alive with the sound of screaming—more alive than it had ever been with the sound of music. *Eat your heart out, Tom Talon,* thought Eddie. When he kissed Monica LaRoche, girls actually fainted in the aisles. Often, the euphoria would drown out dialogue and lyrics. Audience members whom Louis's *Manipulator* hadn't touched were awed by the extraordinary spell this average-looking young man seemed to command over females. The phenomenon was more entertaining than the play.

When Eddie Fanta emerged for his final bow, you'd have thought he was a lead star instead of a supporting player. Two hundred women rising for an ovation persuaded the entire audience to do the same.

Back in the green room, Eddie felt terribly self-conscious. As the other actors removed makeup and hung costumes, they'd frequently sneak a hard glance in his direction. The whole company was as perplexed by tonight's events as the audience had been.

From her makeup table where she removed the thick theatrical stuff and replaced it with Revlon, Monica LaRoche watched Eddie gather his coat and knapsack from his locker. He tried to pass by discreetly, but she wouldn't allow it.

"It isn't right, Eddie."

"Huh?"

"You have to end it, Eddie. You have to make things right again—for everyone. Think of the pain you're causing. For the girls, for their families, for their boyfriends . . . "

Eddie clenched his teeth. She didn't understand this whole thing at all. Thankfully, Mr. and Mrs. Fanta burst into the greenroom and saved him from further reproach. As they smothered him with congratulations, Eddie glanced at Monica one final time. She was pointing at his parents and mouthing the question, "Them too?"

Eddie spun away, putting an arm around both of their shoulders and leading them toward the exit, away from Monica.

"I'd like you to ride home with me, Eddie," Mr. Fanta

insisted. "Your mother brought her own car so I could talk to you privately."

"Okay, Dad."

Eddie's heart started glowing. He knew what his father was going to say, but he wanted to hear it from the man's own lips. For the past few days his parents had been like teenagers again. Dad stayed nights at a Motel 6, but come Mom's quittin' time, he was waiting on the doorstep to take her to dinner or a movie. He always had her home by eleven so she wouldn't be late for work in the morning. Never had Mr. Fanta treated Eddie's mother with a more wholesome and bonafide respect.

As they drove beneath the city lights, Mr. Fanta spent five full minutes torturing Eddie with suspense. At last, he announced, "Your mother and I are getting married again."

"I knew it!" Eddie hollered. His father laughed delightfully to see his son's enthusiasm.

"We should have never parted," Mr. Fanta admitted. "It was the biggest mistake of my life and I'll never make it again."

"*I'll* say you won't," Eddie confirmed. He tapped his fingers on the knapsack.

"It's not going to be easy," continued Mr. Fanta. "We'll have to make a lot of sacrifices as a family. Finances will be tight for a while. Your mother is going to have to keep her job. I may have to keep working in Vegas for another couple months until I find something here with comparable benefits."

"What for?"

"Things are rather complicated at the moment. I haven't filed for divorce from Michelle yet. You have to understand, Eddie, I still care about Michelle very much. In some ways, I still love her—not with the same intensity as your mother but—well, this whole thing is going to hurt Michelle a lot. More than I care to imagine. You see, she's pregnant."

Eddie's expression froze. "She's—" He cleared his throat. "She's what?"

"She's going to have a baby. Naturally, I feel obligated to pay for it. I'll need the insurance I have at my current job."

Eddie's grin melted. His next question was almost a whisper. "It's *your* baby?"

"Of course it's mine." Mr. Fanta grunted defensively.

"Why didn't you tell me this when I was there?"

"We weren't sure how you'd react. We knew your feelings about the divorce were still tender. But that's all over, sport. Everything's going to be the way it was again. I wouldn't have it any other way."

Eddie's eyes turned forward. It was snowing. Flakes were drifting into the headlight beams. The streetlamps overhead seemed as far away as an airplane's tail beacons. Eddie's world seemed to have rushed away at warp-factor nine. Even his father appeared shrunken, withdrawn to an unreachable distance. Eddie was alone. Though Dad continued speaking, further defining the situation like a television weatherman, Eddie allowed the drifting flakes to send him into a trance.

In a pair of oncoming headlights, he thought he saw the eyes of his unborn sibling—bright and pleading—begging Eddie to grant it the very gift he'd worked so hard to achieve for himself. A happy, complete, and—God willing—*eternal* family. *Perhaps*, thought Eddie, *its hopes are as futile as mine.* Maybe this child's parents were simply too intoxicated with the world to ever build anything eternal. One day soon the child might find itself exactly where Eddie was now—groping, angry, confused, desperate—and ever awaiting that final and fulminating judgment of the ages when gods would unscramble the mess some had made of heaven-sealed covenants. A job for gods because only gods could do it.

Eddie might have cried out in anguish, but there was no one to hear, no one to rescue him. This was his decision alone. He trembled because he knew what that decision would be. The unborn sibling would win. If in the end, an eternal family could emerge from the ashes and debris, the blessing would belong to his half brother or sister. Tonight, as soon as Mom and Dad were together, Eddie would undo the spell he'd cast on them. Afterwards, he'd retire to his bedroom and turn off the lights forever on any hopes of see-ing his family as one ever again.

Mr. Fanta's Ford pulled into the duplex's driveway. As Eddie flung the knapsack over his shoulder, his father said he was going to quickly run by his motel room to grab some nonalchoholic wine he'd chilled just for this occasion. Eddie climbed out awkwardly. After watching his dad pull away, he slunk toward the door.

Just his luck, it was locked. Mom had the key. The snow was falling furiously now. He'd have pried off the screen and climbed through a window, but his mother couldn't be too far behind. Eddie folded his knees and sank down on the step, plopping his knapsack in the snow. It felt almost refreshing to treat its contents with such carelessness. For a moment, Eddie considered leaping on top of the knapsack—crushing it all into a sparking heap of high-tech rubble.

Glancing up, Eddie noticed for the first time an automo-bile parked in the street. He might have recognized it the instant he'd arrived except that it was shrouded under two inches of snow. The shape was distinctly Chevette. Eddie stood. The engine and headlights were off.

Eddie retrieved his knapsack and approached the vehicle with caution. He wiped a circle of snow off the windshield. The front seat was empty. Where was Tanya?

With a second glance, Eddie saw her huddled in a blanket on the backseat—sleeping? Eddie knocked on the window. Groggily, Tanya stirred. As she opened the door, Eddie scolded, "You might have frozen to death! You should have at least kept the engine and heater—"

Tanya's face leaned into the light of the streetlamp. Both her eyes were purple and swelling. Her lip was badly cut. She'd been beaten! This was recent—within the last hour!

"What happened?" Eddie demanded.

"Huhhh? Eddie?" Tanya was delirious.

He held her shoulders so she wouldn't fall over. "Who did this to you?"

"You gotta help me, Eddie."

"I will. I'll help. Did Mikey do this?"

With a sudden burst of energy, Tanya dug her nails into Eddie's shoulders. "Please talk to Mikey for me," she pleaded. "Tell him to be nice to me again."

"I'll do more than that," Eddie threatened. He tried to pull away from her—determined to march off to Louis's house and demand the jacket back. But Tanya burst into tears.

"Don't cause any trouble for him, Eddie. Please."

This was strange. Tanya sticking up for a guy she supposedly hated?

She continued, "Just tell him to be nice—to give me what I need."

"What is it you need?"

"Just stuff. He'll know."

"I don't understand."

"Why do you need to understand?" she asked desperately.

"What stuff?"

"Can't you just do this for me?"

"Not unless you tell me what you need from him."

Tanya flew into a delirious rage, her fists flying at Eddie's face. "I hate you, Eddie! I hate you!"

Eddie caught her arms. *She hates me? How could her brain even allow her to say that?* Tanya's body went limp, collapsing onto Eddie's chest. "Tanya?"

He tapped her cheeks with his palm. No response. *"Tanya!"*

Eddie was frightened. Something was terribly wrong with her, but he had no experience in these things. What could he do? Eddie carefully laid Tanya on the back seat and flipped on the dome light. He found her purse. Inside was an empty prescription bottle in the name of one of Tanya's girlfriends. Percodan. Undoubtedly the drug was meant to replace whatever Mikey wouldn't give her. She must have thought she needed everything in the bottle for an equivalent effect.

Keys were still in the ignition. Though he didn't have a license, Eddie tossed his knapsack onto the passenger seat and started the engine. It *would* have to be a stick. He'd only been shown how to work a stick shift once and his dad hadn't been too patient with the lesson. Grinding every gear, he got the vehicle headed in the direction of Pioneer Valley Hospital.

*   *   *   *

Most of cars in the parking lot had left. Duck's sister had told him she might be a little late picking him up, but *man!* Duck looked at his watch. It was almost midnight. The play had been over for an hour. Duck's date, Yen Phok, finally decided to go home with a girlfriend. If he hadn't been ashamed for having forced Yen to stand in blustering snow for so long, he might have accepted their invitation to taxi him home as well. Pride left him perched on the bus stop bench, watching the snow drifts bury his shoes.

Duck almost regretted coming tonight. It was strictly out of loyalty. Eddie Fanta *was* still his best friend—although that title seemed to mean less today than it had only a few months before. Watching all those girls in the audience chanting Eddie's name . . . when Duck wasn't laughing about it, it made him sick to his stomach. Not that he was jealous—Yen was enough for him. Still, he hated what Eddie was becoming: a thoughtless, obnoxious little twerp.

Duck gazed up at the falling flakes, allowing a few to settle on his tongue.

Just then a long Buick with an off-color door screeched to a halt. The Cambodian was drenched by a wave of gutter slush. Duck leaped to his feet, at first more annoyed than frightened. Then a swarm of copper-topped gangsters emerged from the car and surrounded him.

"Need a ride?" Miguel asked.

Without awaiting a reply, three of the Copperheads seized Duck and hoisted him into the backseat. When he was in place, with gangsters on either side, the Buick pulled back into the street. Behind the wheel sat Mikey Swearingen.

"Well, well, well. If it isn't Ho Chi Minh himself," Mikey gloated. "We happened to be driving by and thought you looked a little chilled."

"Do you feel warm now?" Miguel wondered and snaked his arm around Duck's shoulders.

Duck stiffened. "What you people want?"

Mikey repeated his question mockingly, "What do we want? What *do* we want? What we want is some good old-fashioned information. I think you and I have a mutual friend—Eddie Fanta. Am I right?"

"So?"

"He's quite an amazing guy, your friend, Eddie. Might as well call him Eddie Fanta*stic*. The whole community is talking about him. He sure seems to have a way with women, that Eddie Fanta. Half the chicks in school—even my little strawberry, Tanya. In Tanya's case though, Eddie might not find her as attractive as he used to."

Several Copperheads let out a servile laugh.

"What I want to know is, what's his secret?"

"His what?"

"How does he do it? A wimpy slug like Eddie Fanta couldn't make this happen all by himself. I want to know the secret to this scrawny little Samson's strength."

"How should I know? Maybe it his aftershave."

Charmer let out another chuckle, but one glance from Mikey had him clearing his throat.

Mikey addressed Duck again. "No, it's not his aftershave. It isn't long hair either. But *you* know what it is, don't you? You know the secrets behind *all* his little tricks, don't you, Mr. Ho Chi Minh?"

Duck shook his head unconvincingly.

Miguel commented to his leader. "You're wrong, Mikey?"

"About what?"

"His name. It isn't Ho Chi Minh. Let's see, what was it again? . . . Cow? Horse? Chicken? Oh, yeah—DUCK!"

On cue, Miguel backhanded the Cambodian in the nose, drawing a stream of blood. Then he grinned over him.

"Can't say I didn't warn ya."

*   *   *   *

Eddie had been at Pioneer Valley Hospital for two-and-a-half hours when the nurse approached him with word on Tanya. She revealed that Tanya's stomach had been pumped. The girl was sleeping now and would remain so until late morning. Although the prognosis was excellent, Tanya had admitted an addiction to cocaine. The girl was due for serious treatment.

Eddie headed out toward the parking lot. *Cocaine. How could I have been so clueless?* The drug had completely killed the *Manipulator's* spell. In a way, both the drug and the *Manipulator* worked the same way, except that the drug seemed to produce a love exclusively for itself. No sooner had Eddie stepped out into the frozen air when an ambulance backed up to the Emergency Room doors. Paramedics wheeled out a stretcher. Eddie glanced at the victim's face. He did a double-take.

"I know that guy!" he shouted.

The person was more bloodied and bruised than Tanya. He was also suffering from minimal frostbite. His arms were wrapped in air splints. The beaten face belonged to Lu-Duc Ho.

Eddie pried through to his friend's side. "Duck!" he called.

Through swollen eyes, Duck recognized Eddie Fanta. "Eddie?" He spoke with difficulty.

"What's going on? What happened?" Eddie demanded.

"They know everything," Duck said hoarsely. "I told them all."

A doctor pushed Eddie back. "You'll have to talk to him later, son."

As they wheeled Duck away, Eddie cried, "Who's *them*, Duck? You told them *what*?"

"They would have kill me—I *know* it. I sorry, Eddie. I so sorry."

Duck's gurney slipped through the swinging doors beyond the lobby. As Eddie watched his friend disappear, a strange thought roosted in his brain. Eddie felt an undeniable urge to visit Louis Kosserinski. He hadn't felt such a pang since. . . . Eddie's heart started racing. Louis Kosserinski was calling him! Not at any moment during the three weeks Eddie had avoided his aged friend, neglecting him except to put weekly groceries on his porch, had Louis transmitted even the tiniest of neurological signals. Eddie was convinced the only reason Louis would transmit such a signal at this unholy hour was in the event of an all-out emergency.

• *THIRTEEN* •

The blizzard was in remission. But by the look of the sky, smothered by a curtain of clouds whose swags hung just above the streetlights, the snow would start falling again soon. Probably just after daybreak.

It was approaching three-thirty A.M. when Eddie turned the wheel on Tanya's Chevette and entered the idle street where Louis's secluded home awaited him. Eddie pieced together the meaning of Lu-duc's words well enough. This coupled with Louis's distress signal painted an alarming conclusion. There was little doubt Mikey Swearingen and his minions were near.

A quarter block short of his destination, Eddie eased the Chevette to the shoulder and doused its headlights. Opening his knapsack, Eddie pulled out the *Manipulator* and brain wave recorder. He was about to feed his own brain pattern into the unit and pull the lever to the right when a thought struck him. What if Mikey's hatred toward him was so deeply rooted now that the unit was powerless, like it had become with the home teachers and Tanya? Eddie couldn't take the chance.

Instead, he fed the four-digit code for Mikey Swearingen's brain pattern into the unit, pulling the lever far to the left. As soon as the opportunity presented itself, he'd sweep it across the entire gang. A wave of bitter hatred directed toward their leader might well dissolve Copperhead unity once and for all. Eddie abandoned the Chevette. He carried only the *Manipulator*, holding it out in front like a pistol. Wet snow seeped into his shoes as he approached the iron gate, crunching underfoot if he didn't step just right.

The gate was already ajar and the dim light of Louis's porch revealed snowy footprints coming and going.

Stealthily, Eddie headed up the walk. He opened the screen door. Louis's midnight black feline heard him coming and crawled out of a monitor shell, purring like a motorboat. As Eddie turned the knob on the front door, the cat weaved its way through Eddie's legs, anxious to get inside, perturbed that its owner hadn't realized it was so cold. The door was locked. Eddie considered knocking, but he couldn't take the chance of alerting any lurking Copperheads.

The cat followed him around the house to the cellar stairwell. A path had already been trodden and the wooden drop doors were pulled back. The lock on the steel door at the bottom was broken. With a timid push, it fell open. Eddie couldn't imagine anything but Mikey Swearingen's heavy boots inflicting such damage.

Louis's cat, glad to feel the inner warmth, disappeared behind a panel of machinery. The cellar's phosphorescent lights were glowing bright. Swiftly, Eddie hurdled the obstacle course of tracks and gutters to the other side of the room. As he faced the cabinets, the sight which met his eyes made him gasp.

The cabinets had been opened and their high-tech contents were strewn about. Many mechanisms were broken, leaving Eddie to forever wonder what grand miracles they'd been designed to perform.

Most disturbing of all, the metal cabinet—the one Louis described as housing his deadliest creation—sat blatantly open. Each of its six padlocks had been snipped. The steel fragments were scattered about like an animal's bones. Eddie froze. He expected any instant to feel a consuming internal pain which would leave him writhing and dying on the cellar floor. But Eddie felt no fatal blasts of radiation. In fact, the metal cabinet was empty. Louis's *Universal Forces Agglomerative Harmonizer* was gone.

But how could that be, considering Louis's warning? His description of the steel cabinet hadn't been accurate either. He'd said the casing was six solid inches of lead. Yet the walls weren't even one inch thick. Eddie furrowed his brow. *Why would Louis lie to me about something like this?*

"Because," said a voice to Eddie's right, "I couldn't take the chance of having you steal the *Harmonizer* as you did the *Manipulator.*"

Louis was on the floor just inside the corridor which led upstairs. His mangled wheelchair hung over a nearby terminal, hopelessly out of the old man's reach. The cart which Louis used to maneuver about the cellar had been hoisted off the rail.

Eddie rushed to Louis's side. "Are you all right?"

"Of course I'm all right." The old man hadn't given in without a struggle. His mouth was bleeding and a strike to his cheek had split open an existing scar. In spite of it, the tiny receiver remained inside his ear canal, leaving Louis free to perceive Eddie's thoughts.

The boy helped Louis drag his lifeless legs over to the wall and then helped him sit upright.

"I came as fast as I could," said Eddie. "This is my fault. I'm so sorry, Louis. I'm sorry for everything."

"We're wasting time." Louis glanced at the metal cabinet. "We must act quickly."

"What exactly was in there?"

"Exactly what I told you was in there. The *Universal Forces Agglomerative Harmonizer*—a tool which manipulates fate by harmonizing quantum forces, thus charting an individual's greatest personal growth. Your friends from last summer, the ones who attacked you in front of my gate—they tore apart my house and took it with them. Actually, they were looking for something else—the *Chronological Perception: Accelerator/ Decelerator.*"

"The jacket?"

"The one you never brought back."

"I *did*," Eddie defended. "I put it on your porch. Didn't you find it?"

"If I'd known it was there, I'd have surrendered it to them the moment they began snipping off padlocks."

"I thought you said exposure to this thing was instantly fatal."

"I also told you it was a recent invention. That, too, was misleading."

"Why? I mean, why mislead me?"

Louis gripped Eddie's shoulders. "Listen to me carefully. Having failed to destroy that object has become the supreme regret of my life. We have to get it back. Of all the mechanisms I ever invented, nothing can cause more pain and damage. Anyone who touches it will be affected."

"Are you saying this thing actually works?"

"Yes. I never thought it could. I thought I was years from solving fundamental problems. Somehow the quantum reaction self-sublimated when I contained it within a silicon-alloy crucible.

"Yes, Eddie, the mechanism works. But sometimes the course which leads an individual to his greatest potential is far too cruel. If ever one of my inventions tread ground reserved only for God, it was the *Agglomerative Harmonizer.*"

"How do you know it works? What kind of experiments did . . . you . . . ?"

Eddie felt Louis's eyes piercing into his soul. The question lodged in his throat because he knew the answer before Louis could reply. His misshapen head . . . scarred body . . . tearless eyes . . . tormenting pain . . . vanished family . . . forty-year loneliness . . .

"I completed the *Universal Forces Agglomerative Harmonizer,*" Louis declared, "and clutched it in my hands the same day I boarded my private plane with my ten-year-old son for a fifteen minute flight over the Great Salt Lake."

Eddie stood speechless, seized by that piercing stare for an immeasurable period of time. Only when the old man turned away did the boy feel released.

"For the leader of that gang of boys, it's already too late,"

Louis stated. "The *Harmonizer* has no 'on' switch. It's activated by touch, a single nerve ending—a fingertip—against the crucible's shell. He whisked it out of here in both arms as if he'd captured some priceless trophy, ignoring my other inventions, even breaking many of them because I wouldn't reveal how they worked."

"How long ago did they leave?" Eddie wondered.

"Fifteen, twenty minutes."

"I might be able to catch them." Eddie took Louis's arm, lifting the old man onto his shoulders, fireman style. There wasn't much time, but he couldn't leave his aged friend on the cold cellar floor. With his free hand, he carried the *Manipulator*. Louis's weight forced him to drop the unit gently at the top of the stairs. The old man asked to be set down on the old wing recliner in his study. He would await the boy's return. Eddie didn't expect to be gone long. He'd retrieve the jacket from Louis's porch, turn the knobs inward, and then search relentlessly in a slow-moving world for Mikey Swearingen's Buick. Not only would he return to Louis the *Agglomerative Harmonizer*, but after correcting every stroke of damage his actions had caused, he'd return the other inventions as well, vowing never to use them again.

Eddie unlocked the deadbolt on Louis's front door and stepped onto the porch. As he guessed, the jacket had fallen behind the monitor shell. It appeared undamaged, though its surface was ice cold. Eddie hoisted the jacket into his arms, brushing off the dust. As his back straightened, his eyes were blinded by a flashlight outside the porch screen.

Eddie lifted his hand like a visor and tried to count the silhouettes behind the light. It was impossible to tell.

"See, Mikey!" announced the jubilant voice of Miguel. "I told you he'd lead us to it."

"Don't move, Eddie Fanta." There was no mistaking the voice of Mikey Swearingen. "And don't try anything stupid."

The porch screen flew open and six Copperheads entered. Mikey was wielding the flashlight as well as a .38 caliber revolver.

"We thought it was odd finding Tanya's car parked up the street," said Mikey. "To think we were just on our way to pay your apartment an early morning visit. Thanks for saving us a block and a half of travel."

Eddie noticed that Charmer was carrying his knapsack. He'd pulled out the *Translator*. "Tell me how this works, will ya? Your slant-eyed buddy only explained the jacket."

"Speaking of which—" Miguel stepped up to Eddie. "I can take that off your hands now."

"No!" Mikey's voice rang. "Hand it to *me*!"

Miguel glowered at Mikey. Reluctantly, he passed the jacket to his leader chanting, "Sure, Mikey, sure. Just give me second dibs, eh?"

Mikey exchanged the flashlight for the jacket. The Copperhead leader couldn't mask his excitement. "So this is how you gave ole' Mikey a black eye, hmmm?"

Eddie didn't reply.

"Let's get out of the cold, shall we?" Mikey forced Eddie to lead them into Louis's kitchen.

Louis heard them. "Edward?"

Charmer stepped into the study. "Don't worry old man. We got everything under control."

"Where is Edward?" Louis angrily demanded.

"I'm okay, Louis!" Eddie called from the kitchen.

Mikey lit a cigarette and took off his coat, placing the revolver on the table. "Sure. You're okay, Eddie. For the next few minutes anyway. I might need you to tell me if I'm doin' this right."

"Don't count on it," Eddie replied.

Mikey chuckled. "Oh, I'm not worried. Your friend, Duckie, gave us pretty good instructions."

Eddie glanced at the *Manipulator* lying at the top of the stairs, ten feet to his right. Even if he could get to it, what good would it do? Miguel hated his boss already. His best bet might be to leap for the gun on the table. Grinning shrewdly, Mikey kept one eye on Eddie, as if he hoped to see him attempt just that. Having him go for the gun would further justify what the Copperhead leader was going to have to do anyway.

Mikey pulled off his shirt. Slipping the jacket over his head, he commanded two other gang members to strap the wire rods along his arms.

"Funny," Mikey commented. "I once thought this thing was a bullet-proof vest." Mikey's eyes indicated the revolver to Eddie. "I bet you'd like to prove how wrong I was, wouldn't you?"

Mikey should have been looking in the other direction. Miguel was in a better position for testing the bullet-proof vest theory than Eddie. Mikey Swearingen had never considered the impetuous Miguel to be a man of vision. But Miguel saw with radiant clarity what this jacket could mean if it really worked the way the Cambodian described. Until it was proven, Miguel would bide his time.

Mikey stepped back a few feet, giving himself ample room. Miguel moved a little closer to the table and the gun.

"Here goes, gentlemen," said Mikey. "No flashbulbs, please."

As Duck had instructed, Mikey pinched the knobs under his palms and turned them inward.

The jacket sucked up against his skin, startling him slightly, as it had Eddie the first time. But exhilaration quickly overwhelmed his fears. The universe had became a very still place.

As he stepped back toward the table, it gave Mikey the biggest kick of his life to see everyone's eyes still riveted on the spot he'd moved from. Even the smoke from his cigarette floated stagnantly in the air. Mikey swept his palm through it. The smoke adjusted, but as soon as he retrieved his hand, the smoke became stagnant again.

Mikey celebrated his elation by shouting a string of profanities. He looked Charmer straight in the eye. His minion might as well have been a mannequin! Mikey hopped into the study to see how the scar-faced old man was doing.

To Mikey's surprise, Louis had crawled out of his chair, pulled himself across the room, and managed to reach the phone on the bookshelf. He was speaking into it even now. Reaching down, Mikey grabbed the receiver and ripped it out of Louis's hand. Louis's fingers would be badly broken. Not that knowing his own strength beforehand would have inspired the gang leader to be more careful. Mikey brought his fist down on the phone. Though the reaction was too slow for Mikey to perceive, the unit was even now exploding in every direction.

Intoxicated with feelings of omnipotence, Mikey tromped back to the kitchen and twisted the knobs to their original position. "Spectacular!" Mikey exclaimed upon reappearing.

His fellow gangsters had barely noticed he'd been gone, except that he now stood in a different spot and the house was shaking from the weight of his footfalls. A sudden gust of wind hit Mikey's cigarette, sending it and the dish it sat in flying into the wall. Everyone also heard the phone explode and Louis's cry of anguish as he clutched his shattered fingers.

Eddie was tense with desperation. Mikey Swearingen had no idea what he was dealing with—or maybe he knew perfectly well, which was far worse.

"Now it's *my* turn," Miguel demanded.

"Sorry, my friend," Mikey replied. "But maybe I'll leave it to you in my will."

Miguel's eyes became reptile cold. He would collect on that will earlier than Mikey expected.

Again, Eddie glanced at the *Manipulator* on the floor. Mikey noticed the glance, interpreting it as an inclination to escape down the stairs and out the cellar door.

"Do you really think you can get away from me, Fanta? Go ahead and try! I'll send you tumbling down those stairs before you can reach the doorway. Go on! Give it a shot!"

"No thanks."

"What? You need help, you say? Well, all right."

Mikey twisted the knobs. Eddie didn't even have time to acknowledge his own terror when he felt the wind rush out of his guts. His body crashed against the wall beside the cellar doorway. Mikey reappeared to watch Eddie collapse. How amusing to see him writhing, holding his stomach, gulping for breath. Yet all Mikey had done was inflict a love tap.

"Ooops!" Mikey laughed. "Looks like I missed the stairway. Next time I'll have to improve my aim." He stepped up to Eddie and clenched his teeth. "Or maybe I'll just use a full punch and splatter you all over the wall."

Mikey heard metal scrape the tabletop as Miguel snatched up the revolver. Mikey turned. His Hispanic rival was aiming the barrel between his eyes. As Miguel pulled the trigger, Mikey's fingers began twisting the knobs.

He vanished; nevertheless, Miguel confidently cried, "I got him!"

Eddie wondered what would happen if Mikey had really been shot. Would he lie dead in the jacket, his body forever accelerated? In another second, Mikey reappeared, standing face to face with Miguel. The Hispanic had been disarmed. His wrist had been broken. The barrel had been crushed as Mikey grabbed it away. In Mikey's other hand, he gripped the bullet which Miguel had tried to fire at him, having snatched it out of the air.

He held the slug up to Miguel's nose. "Recognize this, you piece of trash?"

Miguel backed up against the table, clutching his broken wrist, his eyes bright with horror.

Smiling like the Cheshire Cat, Mikey disappeared again.

In his unmoving world, the Copperhead leader closed his fist around the bullet, wound up like an all-star pitcher, and let the slug fly. When he turned the knobs back to start, not only had the bullet plunged through Miguel's chest, leaving him dead on the kitchen floor, but a hole was blown out of the wall. "Anybody else feel quite as stupid?" Mikey asked. The other gangsters vigorously shook their heads. Mikey added, "Then I advise everyone to get out of this house! NOW!"

They dashed for the door. Mikey turned to Eddie, still collapsed beside the stairway. The gang leader lifted the cigarette lighter out of his pocket and held it up for Eddie to see.

"Stick around, Eddie Fanta! This is when the party *really* starts to heat up!"

Once again, Mikey Swearingen was gone. It was the longest five seconds of Eddie Fanta's life. The instant the gangster rematerialized in Louis's kitchen, his objectives were treacherously clear.

The room exploded into fire. Flames climbed the curtains, the wall, the furniture, the stairs, as if a great dragon had exhaled its igneous breath throughout the house. Even Eddie's knapsack, which Charmer had left beside the table, was roasting in flames. Mikey had set fire to every combustible surface in the house. Finding flammable liquid in the cellar further precipitated his cause. Had a half dozen fire trucks been in position, there would still have been little chance of saving Louis Kosserinski's home.

In the center of the blaze, Mikey Swearingen, his arms held high, twirled in a glorious circle, knowing full well he could twist the knobs at any instant to escape long before the flames singed a single hair on his head. Mikey had left Eddie a tiny fireless pocket to wallow in until the holocaust consumed him. Eddie knew he was doomed. A warped sense of delight would keep Mikey waiting around until his enemy was completely aflame. Louis's *Manipulator* was only inches from Eddie's hand, but there was no one to aim it at, unless he turned it on himself. A deeper hatred for Mikey Swearingen would serve no purpose now.

"God bless you, Eddie Fanta!" Mikey called over the fire's roar. "You've made me the most powerful man on earth! I'll never forget you!"

As Mikey turned away to admire his fiery creation one final time, Louis's cat sprang out of the stairwell, desperate to escape the suffocating rage which engulfed the cellar. Eddie grasped the *Manipulator*. With no time for careful aiming, Eddie pointed the unit at Louis's cat and pulled the trigger.

The feline's reaction was immediate. It leapt on a chair, using the seat as a launching pad into Mikey Swearingen's face. Mikey cried out as its claws dug into his temples. Staggering, he turned the knobs on his jacket, but accelerating his perceptions failed to dislodge the vicious feline. Mikey reappeared a quarter-second later and clutched at the animal's fur until he could pull it away. After tossing the cat onto the kitchen floor, he found himself facing Eddie Fanta who was in the process of swinging a chair.

The chair impacted Mikey's crown at a force which rendered him unconscious. Using his remaining adrenaline, Eddie hoisted the Copperhead leader over his shoulders and kicked open the burning front door. Flames were licking his skin and raising blisters when Eddie charged out onto the porch and smashed through the screen. Eddie and the unconscious gang leader landed on a cushion of new-fallen snow, rolling to a stop. The cat took advantage of the trail paved by the humans and made its escape as well.

After dragging Mikey a few yards farther down the front walk, Eddie looked back at the blazing house. Louis Kosserinski was still inside. His chances appeared slim, but Eddie had to try.

Anxiously, he loosened the straps on Mikey's chest and arms, leaving the Copperhead's torso naked against the snow. As Eddie stripped off his shirt and breathlessly strapped the jacket against his arms, a police car, responding to Louis's phone call, pulled up to the iron gate. There was another flasher and siren up the street, stopping the other Copperheads in their flight.

Two officers dashed into the yard in time to see Eddie stepping back toward the house.

"Where are you going?" they called out.

"There's someone else inside!" Eddie replied.

"But you can't—!"

Eddie had already vanished.

The welcome stillness of acceleration made it colder than the freezing temperature already prevailing. The glowing house looked more like an array of Christmas ornaments. As Eddie stepped past the burning doorway and into Louis's kitchen, it seemed that fire was not such a dangerous thing. It bore an unlikely resemblance to ice—an entire selection of lemon and orange and cherry flavored popsicles.

On his way to the study, Eddie was forced to step right into a nest of colorful stalactites. He wasn't burned. In fact, the fire felt and reacted strangely like water, molding around his body, but leaving no residue on his skin. The smoke was murky and foglike, hindering his vision, but since smoke was heavier than air, it did little to affect his breathing. All of Louis's bookshelves were aflame, giving the room a sharply toothsome appearance.

But where was Louis? The recliner was aflame, but Louis wasn't sitting in it. And then Eddie knew. There was one more place he could look.

Eddie dashed toward the room at the end of the hallway. Louis was crumpled into a ball in the middle of the floor, unburned, though fire was eating all four of the walls. The mural was indistinguishable now. The flames were licking it black.

Part of the floor had fallen in at Louis's right. Eddie knew in order to move him, he'd have to turn the jacket back to normal. The moment he did, the fire whirled into life, its rage roared in his ears, the crucible heat drenched him in sweat. Louis was stirring.

"Hang on!" Eddie cried and wrapped his arms around the old man's waist.

In that instant, the floor collapsed, likely encouraged by the weight of Eddie's accelerated footfalls. He and Louis began plunging into the cellar's fiery jaws. Louis gripped his own chest. Eddie spun the knobs. The impending disaster froze. Eddie had only to step up about two-and-a-half feet to reach ground level.

Eleven seconds were all that had elapsed when Eddie reappeared in the center of Louis's yard. One officer had returned to his car to find something to cover Mikey Swearingen's bare chest while the other was busy reviving him. The policemen were startled to see Eddie laying the old man upon the shirt and coat the boy left in the snow, but no more startled than they'd been when he mysteriously disappeared.

The nearest officer indicated Louis. "Is he all right?"

Louis was coughing.

"We need to get him to a hospital!" Eddie proclaimed.

"An ambulance is on its way," the officer announced. "Are there more inside?"

"One," Eddie replied, "but he's already dead. Mikey Swearingen killed him."

The police had already pegged Swearingen as the responsible party. Handcuffs were ready and waiting. Mikey had regained enough coherence to make a feeble lunge for freedom. The officers were on him instantly, snapping the cuffs on his wrists. They held each of his arms while leading him out to the patrol car.

Mikey called back to Eddie. "Watch your back, Fanta! Every day of your life! You hear me? I'll be coming for you! Remember my promise!"

The heat of the fire kept Eddie and Louis plenty warm. Eddie was leaning over Louis's face when the old man slowly opened his eyes.

"Edward?" Louis asked softly.

"Don't try to talk yet," Eddie instructed. "An ambulance will be here in two or three minutes."

"It doesn't matter," Louis responded. "In two or three minutes, I'll be gone."

"What do you mean you'll be gone?" Eddie demanded.

"I'm dying." His tone was eerily matter-of-fact.

"Don't be ridiculous! You don't have a single burn—"

He noticed Louis was still clutching his chest.

Eddie started hyperventilating. "Wha—what do you mean? Louis don't tease me like this! Not after all I've been through!"

Eddie sprang to his feet and cried out for help. Over the roar of the fire, no one heard. Eddie dropped down beside Louis again. "Just hang on! The ambulance will be here any second."

Louis gestured for the boy to lean down directly beside his mouth. When he did so, Louis whispered, "Thank you, Eddie, for your friendship."

"NO! NO! NO!" Eddie cried. "Please don't do this to me! Not again! Not again!" Eddie began blubbering like a child—like an eight-year-old child kneeling over his grandfather. They were angry tears. Scalding tears.

Louis whispered again. "My son is waiting."

Eddie gritted his teeth, "You can't leave me yet!"

Louis began to gasp. A choking sound gurgled in his throat. This was Eddie's cue. He twisted the knobs on the jacket inward—four turns!—farther than he'd ever turned them before. The world became so still the air was almost too stale to breath. All the lights seemed to pulse, as if Eddie could detect each wave of photons as it left its source. Now it was impossible for Louis to die. By Eddie's perception, one hundred years might pass before the old man finished that final gasp for breath. *At this rate, Louis might even outlive me!*

But Eddie felt a bitter sting chewing at his flesh. The jacket was so cold it seemed to be broiling him alive. *Pain! Excruciating!* Eddie fell back. Even the snow felt like sun-baked sand compared with the jacket. If he twisted back now, Louis would be dead in a single instant. If he *hadn't* turned the knobs, Louis would *already* be gone forever.

Eddie began shivering uncontrollably. Hypothermia was next. In a matter of seconds, his body and limbs would become irreparably numb. He wouldn't be able to turn the knobs back even if he wanted to.

Eddie gazed on Louis's face. Though gasping his final breath, his features were hauntingly peaceful. Louis Kosserinski appeared free of pain—free for the first time since Eddie had known him. He even wore that same misshapen turn of the mouth which Eddie had once interpreted as a smile.

Eddie Fanta turned the knobs around once, around twice, around a third time. After one final turn, the knobs clicked into position. Eddie drew a deep breath. The flames on the house churned violently again. Eddie looked back at Louis. He wasn't gasping anymore. The crippled old man was gone.

While the heat brought blood back to the surface of his skin, Eddie wept without sobs, his tears melting into the snow. Louis was dead. Eddie was responsible. *Like Grandpa Paxton. Just like Grandpa Paxton.* He regretted turning back the knobs.

Awkwardly, Eddie sat up. His frostbitten skin was stinging. Fire trucks had arrived. Men were dragging hoses through the open gate and into the yard.

There was little they could do. All Louis's inventions, all but this jacket, had been destroyed. There was nothing Eddie could do now to cure his hundreds of victims. They'd have to unravel the *Manipulator's* knots for themselves. Just one more burden of guilt Eddie would live with from this day forward.

The ambulance arrived. Paramedics surrounded Louis's body, declaring it was already too late. Eddie wandered away, passing through the gate. The police didn't see him go. If they needed to ask questions, they could find him later. The Copperheads would surely give them his name. It was twilight now. Dawn was breaking. Snow began tumbling out of the sky again. Just up the street, Eddie noticed Mikey Swearingen's Buick parked on the shoulder. Something compelled him to look in the window. An object sat on the floor behind the front seat, saucer-shaped, about twelve inches in diameter.

There it is, Eddie thought. It seemed wholly appropriate that the most dangerous invention Louis had ever created should also have the most unassuming appearance. No tiny lights. No fancy gadgetry. Just a smooth rounded surface the color of lackluster silver.

A deranged hope welled up in Eddie's mind. Maybe this object—this *Universal Forces Agglomerative Harmonizer*—could balance the tables, equal things out again. Hours after its creation, Louis had become a scarred and crippled shell. Hours after Mikey Swearingen had touched it, he was on his way to what might well be a life in prison. Apparently, the quantum forces of the universe had declared these events necessary for each of their individual progressions. Such consequences were the sort of penance Eddie felt he sincerely deserved.

The Buick's rear door wasn't locked. Eddie opened it, leaned down, and lifted the saucer into his arms. It was after five A.M. Eddie Fanta was virtually sleepwalking. It could be argued that the boy hadn't been thinking clearly. But that would never change what had been done.

With the saucer hugged tightly against his breast, Eddie continued toward home, fading into the heavy blizzard which greeted the morning.

• *FOURTEEN* •

As it seemed, the *Universal Forces Agglomerative Harmonizer*
passed sentence on Eddie Fanta. But it wasn't the sentence
Eddie expected.

Even as Eddie wandered that last half block toward his
home on the morning of the fire, with the *Harmonizer* sealed
in his arms, the boy expected a bolt of lightning to discharge
from the clouds, leaving him permanently scarred and crippled like Louis Kosserinski. He plodded down the center of
the street, tempting the inevitable. An early morning motorist
rolled toward him through the unplowed snow. Eddie shut
his eyes, believing when he opened them again he'd be staring up at a hospital ceiling, his body wrapped in plaster
from head to toe. But the motorist honked, shouted an
insult, and swerved around.

The *Harmonizer's* sentence turned out to be a little more
subtle. When Eddie arrived home, he opened the storage
shed on the side of the house and hid the *Harmonizer* in a
corner where no one would look. When he closed the shed
door, his father was standing there, the keys to the Ford in
his hand. Eddie didn't have to wonder where he was going.
It was obvious the *Harmonizer* had seen fit to shatter the
spell between his parents. Eddie felt cheated. He'd already
determined on his own that such was the best course of
action. Seeing the *Harmonizer* had zapped them back without his help was almost insulting, like a thief whose joy of

repentance is cut short when he gets arrested before he's able to return the money.

Shuffling awkwardly, Dad announced, "I'm going back to Las Vegas, son."

Eddie nodded and looked down, counting the grease stains on the driveway.

Mr. Fanta stepped forward and embraced his son. Eddie stiffened, but his father refused to back off. Instead, he hugged tighter and something inside Eddie started to melt. Hesitantly, his son lifted both arms and returned the embrace. Finally, his father let go. He said nothing more, but climbed back into the Ford and was gone.

Mr. Fanta tried calling Michelle from a phone booth in Mesquite, but the receiver went *click* and the phone ate his change. When he pulled into his driveway, two suitcases and four boxes were waiting for him on the front lawn. For three nights he slept in motels until Michelle agreed to stop shouting and crying long enough to listen to his explanation. He told her he'd been suffering immense guilt for having left his previous family in such a flurry of bitterness. He claimed the time he'd invested in Salt Lake over the past week had resolidified a relationship with his son and got him back on speaking terms with his ex-wife. After two more days, Michelle decided for the sake of her unborn child, she'd accept the possibility that her husband's tale was true. She allowed him back into the house.

The rest of the week following the tragedy, Eddie failed to show up for school. He claimed to have the flu, and his mother, gullible as ever, believed him. An understudy performed his role as Rolf Gruber in the *Sound of Music* for the next three nights. Not that it mattered. Eddie wouldn't have found it nearly as thrilling as opening night. None of his two hundred female fans even showed up. Just as with his parents, the *Harmonizer* decided the spells on everyone else should also be broken.

Louis Kosserinski's only surviving invention, the *Chronological Perception: Accelerator/Decelerator*, no longer worked. Eddie knew it was broken because Wednesday night he strapped the jacket onto his chest with a serious determination to skip three or four months of life. By then, his pain and embarrassment might be forgotten. Besides, he felt an immediate need for a sunny spring morning.

Eddie could turn the knobs on the jacket as far as he wanted, inward or outward, but his perceptions remained the same. Perhaps the jacket had been damaged in the fire. Perhaps turning it so far inward had burnt out some circuits. Or maybe, as with the spells cast by the *Manipulator*, the *Harmonizer* had simply determined that for Eddie's own good, the jacket's powers should be suspended. The *Harmonizer's* powers seemed to override all of the others.

The only time Eddie left his apartment over the next three days was Wednesday morning, when the police took him downtown to help fill out reports on the tragedy, and on Thursday afternoon, when he took a bus to Pioneer Valley Hospital to visit his friend, Lu-duc Ho.

Duck's arms were still in casts. A bandage covered a cut on his chin. Otherwise, he looked unusually cheerful. Eddie had been expecting, almost needing, to hear one of Duck's hellfire sermons berating him for his actions of the past few weeks and months. Instead, Duck cried out Eddie's name, greeting him with all the enthusiasm he could muster. "I glad to see you!"

"You don't hate me?"

"You mean 'cause of this?" Duck indicated his casts. "Ah, I was needing new arms anyway. I wanted to tell you news. You hear already?"

"What news?"

"My mother receive letter from Thailand. A friend hear from relative in Phnom Penh. A prison guard tell this relative that my father still alive. He say my father be released soon!"

"Your father?"

"He *alive*! I *knew* he alive. I *always* knew."

The rumor had gone through three sources. There was a lot of room for error, but Eddie didn't dare express pessimism. Duck had kept the hope alive for eight years. There was something to say for that. Still, Eddie couldn't help but believe, if this rumor was true, it, too, was part of the *Harmonizer's* sentence. What better way for Eddie to progress than by learning to appreciate the reunion of *other* people's families.

On Saturday afternoon the cast of the *Sound of Music* gave a matinee performance, again with an understudy in the part of Rolf. Shortly after it was over, Monica LaRoche knocked on Eddie's front door.

"Are you better yet?" she asked.

"Well, actually I—" Eddie raised a fist to his mouth and faked a few coughs.

"Don't try to fool me, Eddie Fanta." Monica invited herself inside. "I know perfectly well why you won't show up for performances. You're afraid everyone thinks you're a major buffoon because of everything that's happened. Well, I've come here to assure you that the only one who thinks that way is me."

Eddie sank onto the couch. "It's more than that."

"Then what?" Monica demanded.

Eddie remained silent. Though it was all over school that Mikey Swearingen was in jail for murder and arson, the papers hadn't found a reason to mention Eddie's name. Monica had no way of knowing the connection between Eddie Fanta and the charred rubble of a house up the street. But whatever was weighing so heavy on his conscience, Monica was certain that participation in tonight's performance was the best medicine. She sat beside him on the couch.

"You *have* to come back tonight," she pleaded. "Don't make me go through another show with that horrible understudy. He kisses like a walrus."

Eddie looked into Monica's eyes. How could they be brimming with such compassion?

"Why, Monica?" Eddie asked. "Why after all I've done to you, after all the ways I've hurt you, do you insist on being nice to me?"

Monica pursed her lips. "Sometimes I beat my head against the wall wondering the same thing." She stared hard at

Eddie. "There are moments when I've looked at you, even back when I was nine years old, and I swear I know you from someplace. It's eerie. I've always considered myself a good judge of friends. If I really hung out with you in the life before this one, I'm dying to figure out why."

Eddie nodded. Then he looked at her queerly. Had he been complimented or insulted? Monica broke into a wide grin. What kind of game did the *Harmonizer* think it was playing? Eddie would have never expected it to let him retain the affections of Monica LaRoche.

When the curtains opened that evening for Act I, Scene 6 of the *Sound of Music*—the "You Are Sixteen" number between Leisl and Rolf—the performers who emerged from the wings were Monica LaRoche and Eddie Fanta. There arose no screams of rapture as on opening night, but when Eddie concluded the song with, *"You are sixteen, going on seventeen, I'll take care of you,"* the audience responded with heart-felt applause.

Eddie kissed Monica, but it wasn't the kiss called for in the script. Rolf was supposed to break away quickly, leaving Leisl to watch after him with an expression of exuberant shock. She was then supposed to let out a giddy yelp and run off stage in the other direction. Instead, when the kiss was over, Eddie and Monica held each other as tenderly as only teenagers can. No director could have pulled them apart. They remained there as long as the audience applauded, until the curtains were drawn to a close.

* * * *

On Sunday night, Eddie found his mother's address book on the table. The boy felt he'd recognize every phone number inside except one. George Pernyak. This had to be the dude with the 300 ZX.

Five minutes later, Mrs. Fanta heard a knock on her bedroom door. When she opened it, her son was there with the phone receiver in hand. He'd dragged the cord down the hall.

Before the door had opened, Eddie heard a bit of scrambling. In her hastiness, Mrs. Fanta left the very tip of the bottle sticking out from under her mattress. Eddie saw it, but as usual, pretended he hadn't.

"I straightened things out, Mom," Eddie announced.

"What do you mean?"

"George Pernyak. The guy you went out with a few weeks ago. I called him."

"You did *what!*"

"You weren't yourself that night, Mom. Maybe you should give him another chance."

"What did you tell him?"

"I told him you went through a sudden mid-life crisis but were too embarrassed to call back and apologize. He's waiting for your call right now."

Eddie's mother sat down on the bed. "A sudden mid-life crisis, huh? Is that what I've been going through these last couple weeks."

Eddie stepped into the room. "Sure it is, Mom. Just one of those female things."

Recalling details of the confusing week she'd spent with her ex-husband, she mumbled to herself, "It didn't happen the way *Cosmopolitan* described it at all."

Eddie held up the phone again, "Are you gonna call him?"

She shook her head. "I appreciate your efforts, Eddie, but I don't think so. He was nice, but he wasn't my type."

"You're kidding?" Eddie dropped on the bed. "This guy will sure think *I'm* a jerk."

Mrs. Fanta became aware of the protruding bottle as Eddie sat down. Discreetly, she tried to push it under more deeply. When she looked up, Eddie was staring at her. She knew he had seen it. Her expression flashed pain.

Eddie tried desperately to act normal, but it was obvious to each of them what the other was thinking.

Struggling to retain his composure, Eddie explained, "By calling him, I just wanted you to know that as the man of this house, I'll do everything I can to be there for you—to help you and support you. If you want to start dating again,

I'll even help you choose the right guys."

His mother eked out an appreciative laugh, but there were tears streaming down her cheeks. "Thank you, Eddie. That makes me feel very . . . safe."

Eddie's lip quivered. "I love you, Mom. I don't want to lose you. Don't let me lose you."

His mother took her son's hands into hers.

"I don't want to lose you either, Eddie."

They held each other for a long while.

* * * *

On Monday morning, Eddie found the courage to return to high school. One major adjustment pervaded in Jordan View's atmosphere. Copperhead hairstyles had been indiscriminantly banned. Anyone caught with copper-dyed hair was expelled from the school. All former gang members whom Eddie caught sight of in the halls had either dyed their hair a normal color or shaved their scalps as bald as an Idaho potato.

A couple more inches of snow fell that day. Eddie walked home from the bus stop. He brought himself to look through the cold iron gate of Louis's yard. The house had completely burned to the ground. All that remained standing were a few skeletal support beams, charred black. The new snow, so crisp and light, had settled gracefully over every inch of the property. Eddie wanted this to be a good omen. He wanted it to somehow reflect a newness, a rebirth, maybe even forgiveness. But his memory of the tragedy was still too fresh.

Eddie looked down. A bedraggled black cat slipped through the bars of the iron gate. It began purring and rubbed up against Eddie's leg. He lifted the feline into his arms, scratching its neck.

"Bet you're hungry, eh cat? You know, Louis never did tell me your name."

It continued to nuzzle and lick Eddie's chin all the while he carried it home.

The boy started to wonder why the *Manipulator's* spell on this cat didn't appear to have been neutralized. Were animals somehow different from humans?

Every morning for the past five days Eddie awakened dreading that the *Harmonizer's* curse would finally kick in, drumming up some supreme growth-promoting tragedy. Yet each day was the same. In some ways, by small notches, things even seemed to be getting better.

By the time Eddie arrived home, stomped the snow off his shoes, and served the cat a bowl of milk, his curiosity had peaked. Returning to the storage shed, Eddie retrieved the *Harmonizer*. After carrying it into his bedroom, he studied the dull silver shell closely under one of his lamps. The shell had two sections, like a pair of salad bowls set on top of each other. The sections had been fused together, but Eddie noticed a hair thin crack on one edge. He hadn't noticed it before, but it certainly must have been there the morning he took it from Swearingen's Buick. He couldn't imagine something this sturdy having cracked while sitting dormant in the shed.

Eddie shook the unit. For the first time, he heard something jiggle inside. Eddie obtained a hammer and a screwdriver. After three whacks, the saucer cracked in half. Eddie leaned forward to examine the contents. There was nothing but a fine powder three inches deep and a few chips of rust.

The *Harmonizer's* inner mechanisms had completely disintegrated. By the looks of it, it hadn't been a working unit for years. And then Eddie wondered, he honestly wondered, if the unit had ever really worked at all. Even Louis was convinced he hadn't solved some of its more fundamental problems.

But how did that explain Louis's accident and his forty-year vigil of loneliness and pain? And how did it explain Mikey's arrest? Or for that matter, how did it explain the fact that Eddie's father went home to Michelle? Why was every spell Eddie had cast with the *Manipulator* suddenly broken? And finally, how did it explain why the jacket wouldn't work anymore? Was it really only a burnt out circuit?

Eddie lay back on his bed, once again stumped by all the silly puzzles the world seemed eager to present. And then an answer struck Eddie's mind. Sublime and yet perplexing, it filled him with resplendent warmth. For in his mind's eye, there appeared an image from his early childhood. A Fireman from the sky. Perhaps Eddie was no longer Eddie Fanta*stic*. But that didn't matter. His life had been touched by the ultimate "Harmonizer."

So Louis's *Harmonizer* never *had* worked. It was, in fact, the most unnecessary invention Louis's mind ever concocted. He was duplicating a plan already in progress; an eternal and almighty plan in progress since the universe was born.

Eddie smiled. His expression relaxed as he contemplated further.

And then Eddie Fanta smiled again.

About the Author

At twenty-eight years old, Chris Heimerdinger has already changed the face of LDS fiction by bringing it into the realm of endless possibilities. His first two novels, *Tennis Shoes Among the Nephites* and *Gadiantons and the Silver Sword* are now beloved by tens of thousands of devoted fans, young and old.

Born in Bloomington, Indiana, and baptized into the Church of Jesus Christ of Latter-day Saints in 1981, Chris developed his love for story-telling at an early age, completing his first full-length novel when he was eleven years old (a work which he says deserves to forever remain unpublished).

Readers can look forward to the release of two more Heimerdinger novels in the near future. *Daniel and Nephi* is an adventure exploring the possibility that these two great prophets forged a friendship as children in ancient Jerusalem. *Tennis Shoes and the Feathered Serpent* is yet another volume in the celebrated Tennis Shoes saga which will transport our modern characters to the feet of our Savior in the New World.

Chris currently resides with his wife, Catherine Elizabeth, and three-year-old son, Steven Teancum, in Salt Lake City, Utah. A popular speaker for youth groups and firesides, he may be contacted by writing in care of Covenant Communications, P.O. Box 416, American Fork, Utah 84003-0416.